THE SUN MAIDEN AND THE CRESCENT MOON

THE SUN MAIDEN AND THE CRESCENT MOON

Siberian Folk Tales

Collected and translated by
James Riordan

INTERLINK BOOKS
NEW YORK

First American edition published 1991 by

INTERLINK BOOKS
An imprint of Interlink Publishing Group, Inc.
99 Seventh Avenue
Brooklyn, New York 11215

Originally published by Canongate Publishing Limited,
Edinburgh 1989

Library of Congress Cataloging-in-Publication Data

Riordan, James, 1936–
The Sun Maiden and the crescent moon: Siberian folk tales/
collected and translated by James Riordan. —
1st American ed.
p.   cm.
ISBN 0–940793–66–0. — ISBN 0–940793–65–2 (pbk.)
1. Tales—Russian S.F.S.R.—Siberia.
GR345.R55 1991
398.2′0957—dc20   90–42586
CIP

Printed and bound in the United States of America

FOR MY DAUGHTER, NATHALIE

A brother is not only he
Whose face and form are like to ours.
A brother's he who knows our joy and pain
And understands.

Chukchi saying

CONTENTS

PREFACE

During two months in the autumn of 1977 and three months in the spring of 1981 I lived in north-eastern Siberia among the Yakuts, Evenks, Chukchi, Koryaks and the rest. And there I listened to the stories told by people endowed with the gift of words which lent life and color to events long past. I recorded what I could of this precious heritage, and worked in the archives of the Siberian Folklore Institute at Yakutsk. I also used material gathered by my brother-in-law Rashid Davletshin who lives among the Mansi and Khanty in Western Siberia.

There is no space here to describe the many fascinating adventures of that journey; suffice it merely to record one extra-ordinary evening that gives the flavor of this entire labor of love. It was spent in a wooden cottage a hundred miles north of Yakutsk, the home of two Yakut schoolteachers. Our hosts had not been warned of our coming and yet, in an hour or more, the table was filled with all manner of Siberian delicacies: stewed horse's intestines in sour cream, raw fish, pickled apples and mushrooms, black bread, salt, hard lumps of fat, glasses of cream (a sound stomach-liner for the numerous toasts), delicious blackcurrant preserve, and a seemingly endless flow of vodka, brandy, wine and a potent home-brew. Before anyone could raise a glass to his lips, however, the smiling host solemnly dashed a portion of vodka into the fire to appease the spirits.

The evening was unique in that everyone present, except the children, made a contribution in some form of folklore. The host Semyon told riddles and tongue-twisters that lasted five minutes or more; my guide 'Homus John' played the homus (a kind of Jew's harp); one 72-year-old Yakut told stories of the forest spirit bayanai, while another old man, blind and illiterate, recounted scenes from the Yakut epos, the *Olonho*. His was an unforgettable performance. In a sing-song voice, he set the scene for the hero's wanderings. Speaking and swaying to each side, he continued for some twenty minutes before bursting into a high-pitched yodelling song of a maiden weeping. As he reached the song's climax he stood up, tears rolling down his cheeks. All present, including myself, were swept up by the passion of the tale and responded with long rolling cries of 'nooooooooo' and 'that's true' (even though it wasn't!). On a high wailing note, the old bard suddenly stopped and sat down. We then refilled our glasses, drank more toasts to the heroes of the story, and the teller began again. This continued for the best part of the evening (with halts for refills every twenty minutes). The speaker did not drink; in fact, he was so engrossed in the story that he did not seem to notice the flies that settled on his face and hands. At the end of three hours it was time to go, although the storyteller complained he had not finished setting the scene, and the hero had not yet set off on his journey. Evidently the *Olonho* may continue for five or six evenings in a row.

But time is fast running out. In less than a generation the native tellers of folk tales will be no more; literacy and civilization will have overtaken them. So my journey into the back of beyond was exciting and also melancholy. During the evening the young people had switched on the television, having lost interest in the storytelling. Such is progress. Even so, that same progress enables us to share the folk tales of the Yakuts, the Eskimos, the Chukchi and other Siberians. And their stories will be known to far more people than they ever dreamed existed.

We are the wiser.

James Riordan

INTRODUCTION

THE LAND

SIBERIA — whisper its name and icy fingers clasp your heart.

And sure enough, it is a land so chill that in deepest winter you may actually hear yourself breathe as each breath forms a cloud around the mouth that pricks the lips and crackles in the air. Siberians will tell you that if you shout to a friend across a river and he does not hear it is because all the words have frozen in mid-air. Come spring, you can hear what you said as last winter's words melt about your ears!

Siberia truly is forbidding: it contains the coldest inhabited place on earth, with temperatures recorded at more than 160°F below zero at Oimyakon. Yet life goes on in home and school, mine and mill. Only when the winter cold reaches 120°F below zero can Oimyakon children stay home from school; on other days they put on thick layers of clothing and look for all the world like balls of fur rolling down the street. In the two harshest mid-winter months, workmen can take no more than half an hour at a time outside without heading for the warming-up shed. But they have to give up entirely at minus 130°F because machinery breaks down and steel rods snap like twigs in the extreme cold. Such household fixtures as water pose a problem: water in winter comes in huge chunks of ice hacked or sawn from frozen rivers and stored in hollowed caves beneath the houses.

Although the cold is proverbial, there is much beauty beneath the low cold sun in the days of winter: the snow is a glittering bluish-white, the air clear and fresh, the weather dry and crystalline, the atmosphere so still you can hear a wolf howl or a twig snap several

1

miles away. By day the sky is often bright and sunny, while at night you may even see the Northern Lights – the Aurora Borealis – spread across the black heavens like a swaying, shimmering, multi-colored curtain.

But Siberia is not only a land of snow and ice, of wolves and polar bears. In summer, that same Oimyakon turns its face to the sun and becomes as warm as Jamaica on the equator, reaching temperatures of nearly 104°F. Imagine such a turnaround of over 250°F from winter to summer! In the summer of the midnight sun the Siberian plain comes to life; it is warm enough for the bird-cherry tree, lilac and tulips to bloom; the forest floor is covered in a rich carpet of berries; the blue-green forest of larch and fir, silver birch and rowan, is home to the lynx and wolverine, elk and deer, sable and wolf, and the master of Siberia – the big brown bear standing seven to eight feet tall in his furry socks. In its south-east corner Siberian tigers stalk their prey, while down in the south-west the camel is the common beast of burden.

Siberia is as diverse as it is vast. It encompasses three belts of vegetation: the icy tundra, the coniferous taiga forest and the scrubland steppe. It takes up most of the Soviet Union and stretches a third of the way round the world. From the 'Great Wall of Europe', the Ural Mountains, the west where Europe ends and Asia begins, it crosses a seemingly endless plain to the Pacific Ocean in the east, almost within sight of Alaska and Japan. It contains most of the frozen Arctic tundra in the north yet stretches southwards to the mountainous borders of China, Mongolia and Korea. The territory is so immense that nine time zones cross it: when Siberians in the west are going to bed, those in the east are having their breakfast on the following day. At the turn of the century, the only way of reaching the Far East from European Russia was to cross Siberia on horse-back – and that meant two to four years' travel. Even today it takes six days by train and ten hours by plane. Any of the world's largest countries beyond the USSR could be placed with ease within its five million square miles; even ten areas the size of Alaska would not fill the expanse.

Siberia is also a land of great lakes and fast-flowing rivers. Of all its rivers none is grander than the mighty Lena which winds its way for thousands of miles to the distant Arctic Ocean; it meanders through virgin forests, spills outwards at the city of Yakutsk until one bank is eleven miles out of sight of the other, and passes cliffs of red sandstone and even ice in which mammoth and woolly rhinoceros have been found perfectly preserved for ten thousand years.

Some scholars take the word Siberia to mean 'slumbering land', from the language of an old nomadic tribe; others say it comes from the Mongolian word *siber* meaning 'pure' or 'beautiful'. Whatever the origin, Siberia is no longer a slumbering giant, as men and women, settlers and natives, garner its incalculable treasures. By some strange quirk of nature, the riches are embedded in rock-hard ground, for three-quarters of Siberia sits on a thick crust of ice up to a mile deep. The problem for builders is that any normal house will sink into its own morass as its warmth thaws the icy soil beneath. As if that were not enough, Siberia's treasures are located in the most inaccessible places. Gold is to be found in remote Chukotka where winter grips the land in an icy vice for almost the whole year round, where blizzards uproot trees and frosts resound like gunfire. Diamonds lie deep in Yakutia where the cold cracks the earth and shatters steel machines like glass. The best oil and gas are stored in the wastes of western Siberia, where a man may be sucked into swamps and where mosquitoes can drive insane both man and beast. The best furs – sable, mink, ermine and silver fox – are in the ever-menacing forest. And so, too, with tin, coal, nickel, platinum, copper, mercury and aluminum. There are plans by some visionaries to blast away the Arctic ice with thermo-nuclear bombs, pumping out part of the Arctic Ocean into the Pacific, thereby causing the warm waters of the Atlantic to flow into the Arctic. Others counsel caution and respect for the balance of Nature.

Such is the home of the peoples from whom our stories are taken.

THE PEOPLE

The origins of Siberia's natives may be traced down the ages to a time when a colorful human horde made its way up from the warm plains of Central Asia north-eastwards into Siberia. There is evidence in language and folklore of a one-time southern habitation: thus, in some Siberian tongues, the names of months do not correspond to the actual changes of season in the northern climes. The Chukchi, for example, who live at the north-eastern tip of Siberia facing Alaska, call the fifth month *imlihrilin* – the 'month of the waters' (early May), although the rivers of the tundra open only in late May. The Yakuts call April *muus ustar* – the 'month of the melting snow', although snow only melts in north-eastern Siberia at the end of May; March is *kulun tutar* – 'foal birth-time', although mares are not even in foal in that month in present-day Yakutia. Yakut folk tales feature lions, tigers, eagles and camels which have never been seen in the lands where the present Yakuts dwell. A curious creature in Chukchi folklore is a large red-striped serpent which lives near the villages of the dead somewhere in the sky. When hungry, he will attack a wild reindeer, crush it with his coils and swallow it whole, since he has no teeth. After the meal, he sleeps for several days and nothing can rouse him. This is a good description of a boa constrictor. However, since no part of north-eastern Siberia has any snakes at all, the tale, if based on fact, must point for its origin far to the south, where the boa exists.

In their trek northwards, the tribes did not stop at Siberia's boundaries; many crossed from the Chukotka Peninsula into America, for at that time a land bridge some two hundred miles wide connected Chukotka with what is now Alaska, a bridge now submerged beneath the Bering Straits. Once over into America, these primitive hunters made their way south, so that today ties of language, culture and physical appearance still loosely connect the Indians of Peru with the Yakuts, the Indians of North America with the Chukchi, Koryak and Eskimo of Siberia. There is, then, good cause to believe that the ancestors of the natives of the American continent took the icy road across the roof of the world from Siberia into America.

The numerous Siberian tribes existed in a state of barbarism for thousands of years. They hunted seal, walrus and whale in the sea, fished in rivers, trapped fur-bearing animals, snared wildfowl, bred reindeer, ate what bears and wolves they caught, using their hides for clothing and tents. Life was very hard and wretched in the long nine months of winter, starvation was ever at their door and children died by the score. A Siberian adult did well to live till thirty-five and a woman who could raise one child out of every five she bore was very lucky. In times of famine, an entire family might have to feed on a sprat and the bark of trees washed down with bilberry tea; they sometimes even ate their own dead in order to survive – for which the early Russians gave them the name of *samoyedy* – 'cannibals'. They knew nothing of bread or money or soap or linen. They often washed in their own urine, wore rough hides next to their naked skin, ate their own lice, the large larvae of the reindeer-fly, and in summer the herdsmen would pick undigested moss and grass from reindeer dung or even eat the dung itself mixed with young leaves. Their main occupations were hunting and fishing, for which they used bows and arrows, spears and hunting knives. Often they would sit in small hollowed-out boats at a river crossing waiting for reindeer or other game; when the beasts attempted to cross the river they would hurl their spears from both sides, drag their prey out of the water, skin it, hang the meat up to dry and store the rest in a hole in the ground. Reindeer gave them all that was necessary for their simple nomadic existence. Reindeer meat was the staple diet of the inland tribes; from its skin they made a roof for their tents, their clothing, footwear, bedding, cooking pots, sacks and canoes. They hunted on them, carried their homes on them and used them in exchange for other wares. The Yukagir would exchange reindeer for seal and walrus fat and skins from the Eskimos, Chukchi and Koryak, and later for pipes, rings, bracelets and knives from the Yakut.

The only means of intoxication discovered by the natives of Siberia, until the coming of the Russian and American, was the mushroom known as fly-agaric. The mushrooms were usually dried and strung together in threes, which was the average dose. When eaten, they were shredded and chewed like tobacco. Among the Koryak, the woman would chew the mushroom and offer the ready quid to her husband to swallow. Some people would even drink the urine of one who had recently eaten the fly-agaric. It had an effect similar to opium: the person would have hallucinations, see the spirits of the fly-agaric and talk to them; the spirits would take him through the various worlds and show him strange sights and people. The only other slightly alcoholic substance known to Siberians was koumiss – a sour, effervescent drink made from fermented mare's milk and well-known to Tartars and Mongolians.

The main form of dwelling of the Siberian tribes was variously known as yurta, yaranga or choom. The yurta was normally a low mud or clay hut, principally used by the Yakuts. The yaranga or choom varied with the season and habitat, but it was usually a cone-shaped tent (wigwam) of reindeer skin over an earthen floor covered with dog or reindeer skins. There were no chairs or tables; everybody squatted or lay where they pleased round the hearth – the focus of life. Inside the entrance of double flaps, which generally faced the north-east or the Morning Dawn, was a small store-place which also served as a heat lock. This gave on to the outer dwelling room, carefully protected against the cold and the fiercest blizzards. A circular opening was left at the top for purposes of ventilation, although in the harshest winter this chimney was stopped up to keep out the cold draughts, so making the stench and acrid fire smoke almost unbearable. In front of the tent a piece of walrus gut or well-scraped thin reindeer skin was sometimes inserted to admit light.

In the rear of most tents was a sleeping room in the shape of a large box covered with a dozen large skins and with another dozen used as bedding. Each sleeping room was occupied by a separate family and belonged to one woman who was responsible for it. Since it was heated merely by the animal heat of the dwellers, it became habitable only after all the family was inside and the loose lower ends of the cover were tucked in tightly. The remarkable Russian exile, Bogoras, who lived among the Chukchi at the end of the last century described such a room as follows:

The Chukchi sleeping room affords little space for strangers. When guests come, they can only thrust their heads in, lying flat on their stomachs and raising themselves up like so many seals from under the tent cover which is fastened round their shoulders. As these gatherings are usually accompanied by a common meal, and trays of steaming meat and kettles of boiling tea are brought inside, the temperature becomes quite unbearable. The people strip completely or to the waist and their naked bodies are flushed with heat and covered with perspiration. After the evening meal, nobody is allowed to go outside; and so, to satisfy the demands of nature, every person is supplied with a special vessel which the mistress pushes out from under the room cover, and empties on a large slab of snow which lies near at hand in the outer room.

Such was the dwelling of most Siberians even in this century. Indeed, still today some live in such tents, especially in summer when they are with their herds.

The vaulted snowhouse or igloo which was typical of Eskimo tribes did not occur elsewhere in Siberia except among the Kerek, who had not enough wood or skins to make adequate winter houses.

When the brief ten-week summer season arrived, the nomadic tribes would move their herds to summer grazing grounds beside the lakes and rivers where there was plenty of lush grass and moss, and it was warm enough to live in simple lighter tents. Summer was the period of festivities, of weddings and making love. Marriages formed an elaborate ritual, with matchmakers being sent by a youth's parents to the bride of their choice. Among the Yukagirs, it was the custom for a matchmaker to stand before the selected tent and shout: 'Greetings from the family. We are of the same blood, the same body and the same thoughts.' This would have to be spoken three times before a reply would be given and the matchmaker could approach each member of the family to ask permission to the marriage. Should permission be granted, the bride would leave her parents' tent in a reindeer-drawn sledge, her face covered with a shawl. One of the grooms' relations would lead the reindeer, the other men having to shoot arrows into the air to scare off the evil spirits from the bride's path so that her life would be happy. Many tribes strictly followed the tradition that still exists in parts of Asia of the eldest sister marrying before the younger ones could wed.

When a person died, Siberians did not think he had departed from life for good; he had only gone on a long journey from which he would return in another form, usually in the person of a descendant who would bear his name. Bogoras has mentioned the head of a rich reindeer-herding family who died, his name being given to the son born to his daughter-in-law soon after; henceforth the boy was always referred to as the head of the household. When a name was chosen for a child, a stone or bear's paw was often suspended above him while the mother would enumerate one by one the names of all deceased relatives, saying with each name, 'Has this one come?' When the object began to swing, the family would all shout, 'That one has returned to us.' This was common among the Eskimo, Chukchi, Koryak and Itelmen tribes.

As with many primitive peoples, the Siberians thought in pictures and spoke in parables, describing familiar objects with touching beauty. Thus, theYakut call winter 'the season when water dies'; fire is 'the little old lady who opens up her sable wraps' or 'a copper shoe', 'big nose' or 'greybeard'. The Chukchi call bread 'powder meat', mustard 'bitterness', a kettle 'muzzle pot' and brandy 'bad water' (reminiscent of the Indian 'firewater'). The Chukchi calendar distinguishes 'the month of the stubborn old bull', 'the month of the shivering udder' and 'the month of the birth of calves'. The story *The Girl and the Moon Man* lists all the months or 'moons' of the old Chukchi calendar in striking pictures. An acute sense of smell, so blunted among town-dwellers, moved the Chukchi to give onions the delightful name of 'smell grass'. Mutual sniffing, of course, had the same value as kissing among many Siberian tribes. The father, when leaving his family for a hunting trip, would kiss his wife but normally put his nose to the nape of his children's necks and inhale their odor.

Though life was tough in years gone by for the natives of Siberia, they stood up to and survived the cruel ravages of nature. But they could not survive the ravages of 'civilized' man. Some four hundred years ago, in 1581, the faraway 'big white chief', prompted by Russia's richest family, the Stroganov's sent a band of Cossacks under Yermak over the Urals into Siberia. Their quest was the 'soft brown gold' of the sable pelt – the world's most valued fur. This quest led to the conquest of a new world. To the Russians who went forward toward the sun across the desolate wastes, hauling their boats over hill and bog, suffering disease, hunger and death far from home, it was seen as a civilizing, Christianizing and courageous

mission. To the Siberians, the truth was different. For the maraud-
ing, freebooting Cossacks who swept eastwards across Siberia for
their wealthy patrons in European Russia were at one with the
British, French, Dutch and Spanish who were busy swarming into
Africa, Asia and America in search of loot; and ever ready to
murder, plunder and burn whatever and whomever stood in their
way. In just fifty years, the Cossacks had crossed the whole of
Siberia and reached the Pacific, building a chain of Russian forts
from Omsk to Tomsk, from Irkutsk to Vladivostok.

A great number of natives were exterminated by the conquerors
whose guns were more than a match for spears, arrows and stones.
The reports sent back to the tsars are full of remarks like: 'The
native settlement was captured and all the people put to death.'
Some tribes were completely wiped out, others were decimated and
reduced to a pitiful subservient condition. The survivors of the once
proud and numerous tribes like the Itelmen, Evenks, Nenets and
Yakuts, now tributaries of the Russian tsar and impoverished by the
greed of his Cossack tax-collectors, were gradually absorbed cultur-
ally and linguistically by the expanding Russian settlers. Alone
among the tribes of Siberia, the Chukchi put up stern resistance. At
the turn of the century, Bogoras was able to write: 'The Russianiza-
tion of the Chukchi made no progress at all during the two centuries
of Russian intercourse with the Chukchi. The Chukchi kept their
language, all their ways of living and their religion.' In assessing the
'benefits' of European civilization brought to the 'uncivilized' Chukchi, Bogoras admits that 'the first thing brought by the Russians was
a request for tribute and war. But the Chukchi repelled the first and
held their own in the second. Along with all these acquisitions were
also brought contagious diseases like syphilis and influenza, alcohol,
card-playing, and their influence certainly that of the newly introduced inventions.'

Where the gun had failed, three invincible weapons succeeded:
smallpox, syphilis and vodka. Epidemics of smallpox and 'flu carried off hundreds at a time; whole settlements rotted with syphilis;
and those who survived would sell their precious furs and next
winter's store of fish or meat for a bottle of the traders' vodka. And
many would drink themselves to death. It is significant that, in their
folk tales, the Yakuts divide diseases into 'big' and 'small', the

former being imported by the Russians and including leprosy, tuberculosis, measles and influenza as well as the above-mentioned smallpox and syphilis. The 'small' diseases were all local Yakut illnesses.

Where once 'there were as many camp fires on the Siberian plain as there are stars in the sky' (as many tribes say about their past); where once there were over a hundred different tribes living in Siberia; where once several tribes numbered many, many thousands; by the time the Russian Empire was overthrown in 1917, the total number of tribes was down to twenty-five, and some had only a few hundred members. Several were on the verge of extinction.

The new government born of the Russian Revolution inherited the legacy of the old empire, including the Siberian peoples with their medicine-men and their hatred for the white man, their wigwams and their near stone-age economy, their illiteracy and the 'whiteman's disease'. And it set out with good intent to build a new order, a new way of life. The challenge was daunting. When the first envoys of the new regime arrived they even had to invent a language to put across their new ideas: thus communism came to be 'the new law'; Lenin – 'the Russian who invented the new law'; a Communist Party card – 'bearer of the good spirit'; and the Revolution's anniversary celebration – 'the feast of the big speech-making'. In the 'new' folk tales, Lenin and later Stalin took the place of the Russian tsar as 'the Great Sun Chief', who brought the peoples of the Far North the inextinguishable sun whose warmest rays shone where it had been dark, bringing warmth and happiness.

The New Life did not really take hold until people had learned to read and write; and for that they had to have a language. So the first task was to create alphabets and grammars, to open schools and cultural centers. Newspapers and radio programs were started in the native languages as means of cultural revolution and as forums for encouraging people to display their gifts in poetry, song, folk arts, drama and music. This was one way of restoring to the people their dignity and pride, while bringing them into the twentieth century. As an example, the Yakuts received their own written language in 1924 and today their children are taught at Yakut schools in their own language; they have their own colleges and university, their own radio and television (though many programs are, I found, in

Russian), opera, ballet and drama theaters, a symphony orchestra and an institute of the USSR Academy of Sciences studying the folklore of all the tribes of north-eastern Siberia. The Soviet government has, therefore, gone to considerable lengths to preserve and foster native culture – at least where that is compatible with what it sees as progressive values.

The second task of the new government was to restore self-respect among the tribes by ensuring state rights and a measure of self-government. By the end of the 1920s, a number of national areas were established within the USSR: these were designed to prevent the further dissolution of small native populations and their cultures while at the same time encouraging them to develop a modern social, economic and political structure. In fact, they had little or no choice as to what that structure would be, but they were given the opportunity and encouragement to build it by and for themselves. In some cases, their pre-Russian names were returned to them: in this way, the Samoyed became the Nenets; the Tungus, the Evenk; the Lamut, the Even; the Goldy, the Nanai; the Kamchadal, the Itelmen; the Ostyak, the Ket; and the Karagas, the Tofalar.

Another important task of the government was to give the Siberian peoples a sure material footing: it was essential to raise living standards and to put an end to famine and disease. To this end the private fur traders were squeezed out and all the Siberian tribes exempted from direct state and local taxes and tributes. They were given loans through cooperatives and, after 1930, were included in the new collective and state farming system. The individual hunting and fishing gave way to collective reindeer breeding, trapping and fishing cooperatives using modern equipment and veterinary service. With the growth in Siberian industry, construction and mining, a number of northern peoples have also become industrial workmen. Many erstwhile nomads have moved out of their tents into permanent houses of wood or stone in villages and towns where there are nurseries and clubs, clinics and schools, libraries and cooperatives. Slowly but surely they are entering the modern world.

Not everyone would agree on the benefits of the New Life. While many Siberians seem genuinely grateful for what the government has done for them, they would also seem to fear that they may eventually lose their identity and be swallowed up in marriage and

11

custom by the numerically far superior Europeans; they fear that in shedding old discomforts, they are also shedding something of enduring value. Despite attempts to preserve the native cultures, in towns like Yakutsk and Anadyr the native peoples mostly dress and eat and live like Russians, are Soviet citizens first and Yakut and Chukchi second, are normally as much at home speaking Russian as they are with their native tongue. And it is surely only a matter of a generation or two before native speakers become a minority in their own race. There are those who still revere the old ways, but they are few and far between, and are surely doomed: relentless human progress is overtaking them and treating them generally as the townsman treats rustic culture.

Few regret the passing of the old exotic way of life. When all is said and done, it had little to offer the ordinary person. The New Life has undoubtedly far more good than ill. As a Western visitor to Yakutia, Douglas Botting, has put it:

No longer is the Yakut brutalized and his daughter sold into a brothel; no longer is he a second-class citizen, cheated by every trader in town. Today he enjoys the same rights and opportunities as any Russian; he can equally avail himself of the growing number of schools, institutes, hospitals and other essential facilities; he is no longer deprived of the bare necessities of life or of a modest share in the new Utopia; his expectation of life has probably doubled. I never saw in Yakutia (nor anywhere else in the Soviet Union) any child who was hungry, dirty or diseased . . . The boy who yesterday would have grown into a stunted, rickety, illiterate man, looking after cows and praying to the sun, can today become a distinguished scientist or administrator in one of the two most powerful nations the world has ever known.

Moreover, no comparison can be made between the Evenk, Yukagir, Chukchi and Eskimo of Siberia and their blood relatives in North America – the Crees, Chippewayans, Hares and Eskimos whom the Canadian writer Farley Mowat has described as 'debilitated, disoriented islands of human flotsam, nearly devoid of hope and of ambition, surviving on charity – when they survived at all'.

Far from it. The native Siberian tribes are once again flourishing: the Chukchi, for example, have quadrupled their population in

Soviet times, and there are now 13,600 living in their own national area of Chukotka. They have come a long way, perhaps several centuries, in the space of a lifetime.

Today, Siberia has over thirty million inhabitants, most of whom are Russian, Ukrainian, Belorussian and other European nationalities. Only a small number, less than a million, are members of native Siberian tribes. Apart from the Buryats and Yakuts, the biggest of these 'small nations of the Far North', as they are known, is no more than 29,000, while the smallest is only a few hundred strong. All the same, each of them has its own unique language, ethnic characteristics, folklore and national culture.

With regard to language, the Siberian peoples fall into several main groups: the Mongolian spoken by the Buryats on the border with Mongolia; the Samodian (or Samoyed) which is found only in northern Siberia among the Nenets, Nganasan and Selkup; the Finnish spoken by the Saami (Lapps) who live on the Kola Peninsula bordering on Norway and are therefore not located in Siberia at all, but are normally included as a small nationality of the Far North; the Ugrian spoken by the Khanty and Mansi who live just east of the Ural Mountains; the Tungus spoken by a number of tribes (Evenks, Evens, Negedal, Nanai, Ulchi, Orochi and Udegei) living in north-east and south-east Siberia; the Turkic spoken by the Yakut, Dolgan and Tofalars in central Siberia; and the Paleo-Asiatic spoken by the Chukchi, Koryak, Itelmen, Yukagir and Nivkh groups on the north-east and south-east seaboard. The languages of the Eskimos and Aleutians are sometimes included in the Paleo-Asiatic group and sometimes set apart as a separate group. The Ket language is unique in that it is the last surviving member of the Yenisei family of languages which once stretched all the way to south-west Siberia; the Kets now live along the Yenisei River in western Siberia.

These then are the people from whom our tales are taken.

BELIEFS AND FOLK TALES

The folk tales of Siberia are of particular interest for a number of reasons. For a start, they are still being told today in pristine form – and, indeed, believed. In fact, Siberia is one of the few areas of the modern world where folk tales can be recorded from the lips of folk bards. The tales are also unique in that they did not take that journey made by European tales through the realms of slavery, feudal and merchant society. The transition from one society to another inevitably results in a change of former ideas, beliefs and concepts. And it must be remembered that within living memory Siberian tribes were still primitive and godless; their oral folk art had altered little in two thousand years and therefore corresponds to the form and level of primitive tribal society. Hence the folk tales are not tainted with the prejudices and trappings of Christianity and other formal religions, with kings and queens, princes and princesses, merchants and wicked women (witches, step-mothers, ugly sisters and queens). They contain no pantheon of gods; the idea of a god had not yet matured. Nor do they include any historical epos (except among the Yakuts and Buryats) for in the absence of important historical events among the peoples, no legendary hero was needed.

Siberian stories are therefore much more democratic and more truly folk.

So the tales come close to reminding us of our own beliefs long past, our own original concepts of right and wrong, our ideals of love and beauty, the laws of friendship and kinship that have long been cast out of mind and looked upon as unnatural in a socially differentiated society. Siberian folklore shows a strong moral convention, for example, against individualism and acquisitiveness: the meat of an animal slain by a hunter belonged to the whole tribe and was shared among all members of the community – a tradition known as *nimet* among the Even. After all, the very existence of the community might well depend on the success of a single hunter. Every part of the animal meant life and survival, now or later. Among the Eskimo and Chukchi, the bones of sea mammals provided the frame for their yarangas and harpoons for hunting, the skins for covering the home and themselves, the hides for canoes, fat

14

for food and lighting the home during the long Arctic night, intestines for thread. The meat would be eaten and stored in ice holes to be recovered later, often dry and moldy and smelling like old cheese, but nourishing all the same.

The nature of Siberian folklore also reflects the separate forms of economic activity and living conditions on the vast Siberian plain. Several themes and stories contain characteristic detail common to tribes living at the north-eastern extremity of the Soviet Union where the continents of Asia and America almost touch – the Chukchi, Eskimo, Kerek, Itelmen, Koryak and Yukagir, as well as tribes across the Bering Straits such as the native peoples of northwest America. We must assume that this similarity comes from close contact and kindred origin in the past, in addition to similar precarious living conditions in the most northerly area in the world. The tales of rude and primitive people living in a world of boundless tundra stretching beyond high, bare mountains with an ice-cold sea crashing against the cliffs cannot be so rich and elaborate in description as those of pastoral groups like the Yakut, Buryat and Saami. The material is limited by the nature of their experience. No Eskimo or Chukchi could recount tales of the great forest or of life in which people dug the ground to make plants grow. Their folklore is more stark and grim, though with a fantastic beauty of its own. North Siberian folklore deals in plain words and goes straight to the point, sometimes lending the story a very vivid and realistic character.

All Siberian tribes shared the belief that everything that moves is alive. Darwin once likened this attitude to the dog which barks at an open umbrella moved by a breeze. And Bogoras says of the Chukchi that they 'will take for living the tree that rustles, the wind that passes by, the stone that waits silently lying upon the ground but makes the passing man stumble over it, the lake, the river, the brook, the hill that towers over the plain and throws its shadow upon it'. A spirit lurks in every stick and stone, tree and animal; and each object may take another form with gay abandon: the girl hiding from the moon changes into a mound of snow and a lamp or can turn into a block of stone, a hammer, a tent pole, a hair on the tent flap or a grain of soil (see *The Girl and the Moon Man*). Every object can act according to its own will and has its own separate

existence (*gekulilin*, as the Chukchi says – 'it has its own voice').
Even the chamber pot (and its contents!) has a separate land and
house and its own language.

This form of understanding arose as a direct expression of man's
feeling of impotence before the mysterious, powerful and terrible
forces of nature. As in the story *Kotura, Lord of the Winds*, long
blizzards prevented hunters from gaining food, led to hunger and
total darkness and cold. The storm could at any moment sweep a
man into the tundra or tear off a chunk of ice and carry him out to
sea. No less disastrous was a poor catch of fish or land animals.
Hunger and death from starvation were the constant companions of
natives of the Far North, and people supposed that cruel spirits were
always the culprits. Being wholly dependent on nature, they did not
divorce themselves from it, and their fear of it caused them to
attribute supernatural powers to natural phenomena. Man may
struggle with natural objects and vanquish them; he may sacrifice to
them and ask them for protection. He may pick up the smaller ones
and use them as charms. These charms or spirits of the objects – a
swan's beak, owl's or bear's claw, piece of walrus tusk – carried
about the body would ensure him of safety against all hostile forces.

Life under such circumstances would have been an endless fata-
listic round of terrors had there not been some defense against the
evil spirits. The various charms, chants and sacrifices, even folk
tales, provided hope in countering the forces of destiny. But the
main defense was the medicine man or shaman. He alone had the
power to commune with the spirits, to mediate between them and
ordinary mortals, to talk with the souls of the dead on behalf of the
living. The shaman was often an extraordinary character both in
physical appearance and in acting talents. He would be a mystic,
poet, sage, healer of the sick, guardian of the tribe and repository of
its folklore. The best were skilful ventriloquists who could throw
their voices to all parts of the tent; artful impersonators who could
make their audience fervently believe that other beings, often in
animal shape, were present; brilliant illusionists who could conjure
up insects and clumps of blood from their own bodies or from those
of the sick.

To become a shaman, training and practice were relatively unimportant; a person had to 'receive the call', to suffer a religious experience and be initiated into the mysteries of the art. By his symbolic death and resurrection, he acquired a new mode of being, his physical and mental frame underwent a thorough change. Sometimes men became 'women' and women became 'men'. During this period of initiation, the novice would see the spirits of the universe and leave his body like a spirit, soar through the heavens and the underworld. There he would be introduced to the different spirits, taught which one to address in future trances. Not only the spirits of the shaman's ancestors, but many other spirits took part in initiating the future shaman; they included, among the Nganasan, the spirits of water and earth and even of 'smallpox', who was considered to be a Russian female spirit.

Since sickness was thought to be caused by an evil spirit entering the victim's body, it followed that the shaman could call it out and cure the patient. He would do so by a special ritual: he would beat a rhythm on his drum, sway and sing, gradually increasing the sound and interspersing it with long-drawn-out hysterical sighs, growls, groans and satanic laughter as he went into his ecstatic trance (see the Chukchi tale *Tynagirgin and Gitgilin*). He would often imitate the chattering and shrieking voice of the spirit as it entered or left his body, and the cries of various animals and birds which were supposed to be his assistants. In the darkness, the effect was often very frightening with the whole tent shaking from the shaman's shenanigans. The audience would often have the fear of a thousand devils put into them.

A shaman could be of either sex or even of indeterminate sex. Some scholars who have studied shamanism have mentioned the reverence paid by tribes to those among them suffering from physical or psychic diseases or from some form of deviant conduct that sets them apart from the group. These are the people who frequently became shamans. This is not unlike the awe in which 'simpletons' are held in old Russian beliefs, or even the peculiar mixture of inspiration and madness that has marked the careers of prophets and mystics in some religions. On the other hand, there is little doubt of the great skill and intelligence of many shamans which gained them such a hold over the tribes and made them the wealthiest members – they did not work for nothing after all.*

Siberian folk tales fall into three distinct groups: tales of the world's creation, tales of the spirits and everyday life, and animal tales.

Tales of the Creation

Most northern peoples believe that there are several worlds, one above the other so that the ground of one is the sky of another. Some are above the earth, others below it. Each one has a hole in the top of the sky, usually at the foot of the polar star; the shamans slip through this hole when moving from one world to another. The heroes of a number of tales fly up through this hole, and people of the upper world may look down through the hole upon the lower one. In the Chukchi story *The Eight Brothers*, a young man is shown the lower world through a hole in the ground of the upper one; seeing the family he has left behind, he drops a tear and at once sunshine turns to rain upon his kinsmen below. He returns by being lowered on a strap (in other versions, on a spider's thread capable of bearing the weight of twenty reindeer-loads). In other Siberian tales, the gradual rise of the road leads to the sky. It can also be reached along the path of the rainbow (see the Nivkh tale *Brave Azmun*) or by flying up in the smoke of a funeral pyre (see the Saami tale *How Happiness Came*).

There are different views on how many worlds exist: the Chukchi believe in nine, the Yakut in seven and the Evenk in three. To the Chukchi the worlds are alternately peopled by men and spirits, the lowest world being inhabited by those who have died twice and therefore cannot return to earth. To the Evenks, the upper world or

---

* It is small wonder that they opposed change so vehemently, particularly that involved in schooling and cooperative herding in Soviet times. Although they seem to have preserved their influence up to the early 1930s, they were then mostly rounded up at the same time as the kulaks (wealthy farmers) whose fate they shared. That they have not entirely vanished is evident from the much-respected and well-remunerated men who today perform as shamans in Siberian folk ensembles in the USSR.

ugu buga is populated by powerful supreme spirits, masters of the elements, animals and people, while the lower world is inhabited by evil spirits. Of prime importance among the supreme spirits to the Evenks is the sun, Dylacha, master of warmth and light. To other peoples (Saami, Nenets, Koryak), the sun is thought to be a living being clad in bright garments who pastures his deer and drives around the sky as a nomad in a sledge or sleigh pulled by dogs or reindeer. The sun can descend to earth on one of his rays and ride about on his copper-red reindeer. The primitive people thus ascribe to heavenly bodies their own way of life, nomadizing with herds of reindeer across the tundra.

The moon is either man or woman (sometimes the sun's sister or brother), though in some tales is referred to as the sun of evil spirits; shamans apply to the moon for evil spells and chants. But despite his great powers, the Moon Man's attempt to carry off a Chukchi girl in *The Girl and the Moon Man* is foiled and she proves stronger than him. The Chukchi here also invent a delightful story about the moon who has to create the seasons of the year as a ransom for his freedom.

Dawn and Twilight also play an important part in northern mythology. The two are said to live together with a single woman stolen from earth. They appear in the Chukchi story *Tynagirgin and Gitgilin*, in which a young shaman ascends to their dwelling in the upper world to take the wife for himself and enters into a shamanistic contest with the two giants. The story gives an interesting insight into polyandry, which was at one time common among northern hunters: when nomad men went hunting for months on end they would sometimes take a shared wife with them.

The stars and planets also have their various interpretations. To the Evenk the visible blue sky is the taiga of the upper world in which lives the great elk Keglun. In the daytime the elk goes into the thickets of the heavenly taiga and therefore is invisible from the land of people. At night he comes out on to the mountain peaks and, being the most powerful of the dwellers (stars) in the heavens, he may be seen by people from earth. He is in fact identified with the constellation of the Great Bear, while his calf is the Little Bear. The Saami have a similar notion of the elk, Golden Antlers. This is also reminiscent of the Eskimo conception of the Great Bear being a giant elk looking down on earth. Other tribes, too, have their captivating tales about the sky and the stars which reflect their own herding or fishing existence: like the Saami story of the Milky Way (see *The Silver Maid*) and the Chukchi view of the Milky Way as being a pebbly river with many islands. The Northern Lights are believed by many to be a special world inhabited by those who died in violence. The red glare is their spilled blood and the changing rays are the dead souls of children playing ball with a walrus head. Others, especially the Eskimos, saw the Northern Lights as images of their own families and friends who had passed out of this world and were now dancing happily around fires in the heavens. In the lovely Saami tale *Daughter of the Moon, Son of the Sun*, they are brothers engaged in mock battle in the sky at night but who return to earth to sleep during the day.

There are a number of tales connected with the creation of the world, of light and of people. In one popular version, the raven – variously called the Creator's outer garment or the Creator himself from which the Eskimo and Chukchi are descended – sends several birds towards the dawn to try to pierce the stone wall of the day with their beaks. One of the birds, a wagtail in some versions, succeeds in making a small hole and the light of dawn passes through. The raven drops some seal bones on the earth and they become the first man and woman. The reindeer-herding Koryak say they were made from two reindeer brought by a shaman from the uppermost world; they also say disparagingly about their seaboard neighbors, the maritime Koryak, that they arose of their own will from dog excrement!

Tales of the Spirits and Everyday Life

Most northern tribes have no conception of a god or a supreme spirit. There are many spirits, some good, some bad, some powerful, some weak. Bogoras designates three classes of spirit common to north-east Siberian tribes. The first are evil spirits who walk invisible over the earth, producing diseases and preying on the human body and soul. These spirits are always described as a tribe of beings living very much like tribes of men: they reside in villages or camps, travel with reindeer and dogs, marry, have children, need food and obtain it by hunting mortals with harpoons and nets. Human souls are like fish or seals to them. They are very dangerous, yet at the same time not immune from attack by mortal shamans, who can just as easily kill them as they kill men. Like the 'big' diseases of the Yakut, mentioned earlier, they usually come from beyond the tribal lands. A number of tales feature such disease spirits as Cough, Colic and Nightmare; the latter has a black face and strangles men at night, drinking the blood from their throats. Epilepsy lives underground and strikes men sleeping alone in the tundra; and Syphilis is represented as small crimson people moving around with tiny red reindeer herds and hiding in cloudberries, who come to human settlements and make their camps on human bodies.

The second class of spirits are earthly tribes hostile to the tribe, and are more or less fabulous. They live by hunting seal and are always poor and hungry; they are also cannibals. The third class of spirits are those that come at the call of the shamans and help them in their magic. Although they live in tribes and camps, they come to the shamans singly. They are mostly natural objects such as wolves, reindeer, walrus, whales, plants, icebergs, winds and even household objects such as pots, hammers, needles, the chamber pot and excrement.

All kinds of spirits are believed to be small, no bigger than a man's finger. And they may be rendered harmless by being struck with the hand or a knife. Thus, in the story *The Eight Brothers*, the youngest brother kills the insect spirits with his hand; in that same story, the mosquito people are evidently the souls of the dead who emit sounds like the humming of a mosquito, bee or beetle. The Chukchi call spirits the *kelet*; the Koryak, *kalak* or *nynvit*; the Eskimo, *tornirak* or *tungak*. The Yakut *abaasy* can take various forms and usually appear at night, being unable to bear the daylight.

Besides spirits, several other monsters roam through Siberian stories. The Chukchi have the giant polar bear who on stormy nights imitates the cries of people in distress, lures them to their doom and then devours them. The Yakut have the one-eyed monster Greedy Mogus who specializes in eating little children. The Saami have the terrible Clayman who can devour anything whole, from boats filled with fishermen to milkmaids with their cows and pails. The Evens have the one-eyed, one-legged, one-armed giant Choleree, while the Evenks have the flying man-eater Korendo. Happily, all these monsters can be defeated, even by children. Children are particularly susceptible to the preying wiles of spirits and monsters. Among the Yakut there is the obsession with evil spirits who constantly shadow a child from the moment it is born, with the sole purpose of inflicting disease and death upon it. The rearing of the child is fully centered on the struggle against the spirits. In families where children have died, the newborn baby is often given an animal, bird or even rude name (such as 'dog's bottom') so as to make it repulsive to the spirits. The mother does her utmost to protect the child from evil spirits, sings special lullabies to it, hangs a bear's or rabbit's paw over the cradle and a bear's tooth around its neck.

The many stories featuring orphans are a reminder that, in the grim fight for existence, tribes sometimes had to abandon a child or deliberately cause the old and infirm to freeze or starve to death. Several Siberian tribes practiced 'voluntary death', when an old man or woman, feeling no longer useful, would ask a close relative to suffocate or stab him. No one saw any great cruelty in this; should the old people refuse to submit, they lost respect and were despised. Young children, too, were sometimes put to death when their fathers died because they had lost their source of food and left the intolerable burden of an extra mouth to feed on the rest of the group. It was an absolute necessity when living as a small band searching for enough food to eat that when things got really tough the weaker members should be sacrificed for the welfare of the whole community. Nevertheless, hopeful stories abound where the abandoned orphan finds a new life on his own in another land.

In an environment so dominated by the elements, it is natural that many tales should interpret the weather in a fantastic way. Like the American Indians, the peoples of the Siberian Far North imagine thunder to be a mighty bird. The Evenks, for example, speak of it as a great Thunder Bird, the rustle of whose wings is heard on earth. They make a wooden image of the bird and fix it outside their tents on a long pole. It is believed to protect the soul of the shaman who may encounter many dangers in his flight through the air. They see proof of its powers in lightning-damaged trees which it has torn to shreds with its 'claws of stone'. The eastern Nenets liken the Thunder Bird to a duck whose sneezing is said to be the cause of rain. Among the Chukchi and Eskimo, thunder is said to be the rattling noise made by girls in the upper world playing on a spread sealskin. Rain here is not portrayed as their tears or even as water when they wring out their washing, but, less romantically, as their urine. In fact, urine is generally believed to have a protective quality, which is why, in the story *The Eight Brothers*, the young man is told to stand on the spot where urine is emptied – so that nothing untoward will happen to him.

Hail is the stone of thunder which falls from the sky in round balls or even in the form of roughly chipped arrowheads and spears. Cold winds and blizzards are produced by a giant who lives on the borders of our earth and who spends his time shoveling snow from his dwelling (see the Nenets story *Kotura, Lord of the Winds*. Sometimes the winds have an old mistress who causes snowstorms by shaking the snow from her tent (see *Bold Yatto and his Sister Tayune*). The telling of certain folk tales is supposed to cause good weather, which is why some tales end with 'There! I have killed the wind (or storm)!' In stormy weather, people had little else to do but huddle together in the cold and darkness and keep their spirits up by telling stories until the storm abated.

Animal Tales

The most popular form of Siberian folklore are the short stories, often based on dialog concerning animals. In the severe conditions of the Far North, after all, hunting animals was the main occupation and the sole condition for survival. The difference between man and beast was regarded as slight and surmountable. In countless tales, it is related how certain animals were once human beings and vice versa. The Buryats say of the bear that he was once a hunter or a shaman who was changed into a bear, and they tell of a land where men are born as large dogs; even fish such as the burbot are human beings who have been drowned. The Evenks believe that when the beaver was a human being, he was a skillful archer. The Nanai take the tiger as their forbear. The Kets say the swan was originally a woman who still, of course, experiences menstruation. The Yakuts believe that women descended from cranes. Animals can marry humans and the children of such unions possess a human intellect combined with animal strength (see the Yukagir story *Man-Bear*).

Animal tales were sometimes told during the hunt when a blizzard forced the hunters to take shelter; and then the story-teller would speak loudly because it was generally thought that animals listened to the tales as well. Typically, few tales were told of domestic animals like the dog, cat, goat, sheep, rooster, cow or horse, since whatever did not serve as an object of the hunt had little interest for the hunting tribes. Some, indeed, had no names for creatures that were not hunted. The most common actors in the tales are the bear, fox, wolf, wolverine and, of course, the raven (see below). Whereas the tales about spirits reflect man's fear of the unknown, in the animal tales man often enjoys a close friendship with the animals; though they are the object of the hunt, they are not man's enemy. Even when game is killed it was not thought an offence against the beast, insofar as it had come as a guest of its own accord. The slain beast was highly praised and persuaded not to be offended, but to return again to the hunters another time in another form. For that to happen the hunters had to offer sacrifices: they would cut off small pieces of the animal's nose and throw them on to the ground or back into the sea, all the while muttering thanks and pleading for it to come back again.

Some animal tales are told by old women to children who first get their knowledge of animals in this way. And when they ask, why an animal is such a size, shape or color, the folk tale provides an answer (see *The Cuckoo and Why Hares Have Long Ears*).

The cult of the bear has a special place in Siberian folklore, largely from his believed kinship with man: he alone among the animals is believed to possess a soul like man's and to understand the language of both man and other beasts. The Evens and Evenks actually believe themselves to be descendants of the bear or of a bear-faced boy. The Khanty call the bear 'old man in a fur coat', while the name 'grandad' or 'old man' is used by several other tribes. The Mansi also refer to the bear as 'forest woman' or 'mountain woman'. The Ket say that his skin is only a cloak under which is a being in human shape endowed with divine power and wisdom. It is interesting that, even in this century, if a Ket man had to take an oath before a Russian court, he would take it on a bearskin, believing that the bear in the forest would not fail to punish him if he swore falsely. A common custom among some tribes was to rear bear-cubs: after killing the she-bear, they would take the cubs home and give them to childless families where they would be cared for like children. In the hunting season, the tame bear would be taken to the forest where he was supposed to give warning if he smelled the presence of wild bears.

The most frequently recurring creature in animal tales is the raven. He holds a special place in Siberian mythology, just as he does in that of the North American native peoples. The raven, and sometimes the spider, is considered to be a sacred being, the creator of the universe, and representative of age and wisdom. Killing him is taboo. The raven is thought to have helped create the earth, all animals and humans; he brings light and fresh water, teaches the human race the ways of earthly life – from making nets to having children. At the same time, he is the common laughingstock, foolish and even somewhat lascivious (many raven tales, omitted here, would be considered far too bawdy for 'modern' children); he plays tricks on others and is also the butt of various tricks. The folk name for the raven is similar in several Siberian tongues, evidently originating from the Itelmen word Coot (Cookki in Kerek, Coshkli in Eskimo, Coorkill in Chukchi, Cootcoonnekoo in Koryak). His wife is known as Mitti and their son as Ememcoot. In the desolate landscape where the north-eastern Siberian tribes roam, the cry of the birds, especially the raven, can be the most noticeable sign of other living beings in the vicinity. It is not to be wondered at therefore that people would revere a bird like the raven, might call to him and receive answers back. His black color also singles him out from other birds: this is explained in folk tales by his quarrel with an owl, seagull or loon, in which he has black paint or soot thrown over him.

THE STORYTELLERS

The oral art of a people without a written language is a vital source to sustain their courage and sanity. That is why, in the cold and dark of the long winter days and nights, the storyteller was such a welcome guest in any family. It is hard to overestimate his importance in the lives of people who had no other spiritual sustenance. The modern Yakut poet Semyon Danilov once expressed it to me as follows:

'I was born in a land where there were fewer people literate than there were blind and lame. In my remote and inclement land, for us children living in "deaf" yurtas scattered like tiny islands in an ocean of taiga, folk tales recounted to us in the long winter evenings were everything. They were our nursery and school, radio and television, newspapers and books. Yakut children had to work early, as soon as they could walk; and they worked all day long, impatiently awaiting those cherished moments of an evening when Grannie or Grandad would sit closer to the fire, pull a rabbit-skin rug round them and begin a story. Thus began that treasured hour of storytelling. The stories taught us to understand and love the beauty of life, to be brave and to fight evil. And now, when I recall my cold and hungry childhood, I wonder what life would have been like for little children if it had not been for those wonderful fantastic stories . . .'

Those words help us to understand the value that folk tales and their tellers had in the lives of Siberians. There were some in whose amazing memories were recorded thousands of lines and hundreds of tales – and they would believe every word they themselves retold. The great Yakut bards – the olonhosuts – could recite up to fifteen thousand lines of the folk epos, the *Olonho*, and go on for several days and nights at a time.

The first recorders of Siberian tales were Russian political prisoners, men and women exiled to Siberia by the tsarist regime. Such men as Ivan Khudyakov (1842–76), son of a West Siberian teacher, and arrested in St Petersburg in 1866 over the assassination of Alexander II; this proponent of Narodnik or populist ideas was exiled for life to the cold and privation of Verkhoyansk, where he lived in the crowded yurta of a poor Yakut. He survived just three years, soon driven mad by the conditions, and died in the Irkutsk mental asylum at the early age of thirty-four. Before his death he had learned the Yakut language, written a Yakut alphabet and grammar, and gathered a wealth of Yakut folklore, including the epic

Olonho. His work was published posthumously as *The Verkhoyansk Collection* in Irkutsk in 1890, the first ever book of the folk tales of a Siberian people.

Another populist, Vladimir Jochelson (1855–1937), born in Vilnius on the Baltic, was exiled in 1888 to the Kolyma region of Yakutia where he was allowed to take part in the Russian folklore expedition of 1894–6 (since he knew the Yukagir language and customs). Subsequently he studied the cultural and historical links between North America and north-eastern Siberia, and collected folk tales of the Koryaks, Aleutians and Yukagirs. He survived his exile and emigrated to the United States in 1922 where he spent the last fifteen years of his life.

The most remarkable of all political-exile folklorists was Vladimir Bogoras (1865–1936). Born near the old Russian town of Rostov, he became involved as a young man in the Russian populist 'Land and Freedom' revolutionary group and soon followed his fellow Narodniks into Siberian exile. During his eight-year period in Kolyma he learned the local languages, particularly that of the Chukchi, was included in two important folklore expeditions, and even changed his Russian name to Tan. During the joint Russian-American Jesup North Pacific Expedition of 1900–1, he gathered some five hundred folk tales from the tribes of north-eastern Siberia, mostly from the reindeer-herding and maritime Chukchi. His study of the way of life of the Chukchi, with whom he shared part of his life, is one of the most detailed and exciting anthropological works ever undertaken. Not only did Bogoras record more lore and information on the peoples of Siberia than any other person, he passionately devoted his life to the protection of their cultural heritage and integrity. As initiator and director of the Committee on the Far North in Soviet times he worked on behalf of the Siberian peoples right up to his death in 1936. It was under his influence in particular that serious studies and collections were made of Siberian folklore, and that a special folklore institute was established in Yakutsk.

It was the very lack of a written language that helped to promote folk tales, the sole means of expressing the ideas and aspirations of the common people. Ironically, it is the spread of literacy that is steadily extinguishing that oral tradition. The old storytellers are passing away, and the children now often prefer television, or books by Chekhov, Dickens and their own Siberian authors. And yet the Siberians have also gained very significantly from modern living. Unlike the native peoples of North America and Greenland, the natives of Siberia have developed, through a written language and literacy, a great new literature of their own; they now have their own poets and writers, well known in their own country and even far beyond – like the Chukchi Yuri Ritkheyu, the Yukagirs Uluro Ado and Tekki Odulok, the Nivkh Vladimir Sangi, the Yakut Semyon Danilov, the Koryak Ketsai Kekketyn, the Mansi Yuvan Shestalov, the Nanai Grigori Hodger and a host of others.

This is progress to be justly proud of. But literacy has meant something else: for those wonderful treasures of folklore accumulated down the centuries can today be read and enjoyed by all Siberians – and by us as well.

JAMES RIORDAN

MY DEAR LITTLE DEER

My dear little deer,
Darling little deer,
My shy gray friend,
My fleet-footed friend,
My Far Northern friend.

What dear little horns
You have.
What soft little ears
You have.
What a warm little nose
You have.
What a funny little tail
You have.

Adorable little deer,
Where have you been, my gray one?
Where have you been, my sleek one?

Dear Mistress mine,
I've been far away
O'er hills and ravines
To the land of new grass.

My dear little deer,
So be it, then go
Where the moss is green
And the grass is new.
Only come back soon
When the moon is full.

Fear not, Mistress mine,
I'll eat my fill
Of the tender spring grass
And return once more
To my home with you.

AKANIDI THE BRIGHT SUNBEAM

The Sun has many children: his eldest son Peivalke, the four Winds, the Storm Cloud twins, Lightning, Thunder and Tempest. But most of all the Sun loves his three daughters: Golden Sunshine, Misty Shadow and his youngest daughter Bright Sunbeam.

The Sun's daughters live proud and free chasing wild reindeer over the tundra, dancing in woodland glades, flitting like silver fish in Lake Seityavr and resting on its broad banks.

One day, the three sisters spied a birch-bark boat come gliding across the lake; and in the boat was a fisherman casting his nets into the water. Half the lake fish seemed to seize the nets so that it would surely take five strong men to pull them out; yet the young fisherman took hold of one end of the nets, strung it over his shoulder and hauled it easily into the boat.

The sisters followed the fisherman's movements and hid among the trees. When he had brought his boat ashore, hung up his nets to dry and eaten his fill of the fish, he fell asleep by the lakeside.

Thereupon the eldest sister, Golden Sunshine, stamped her foot.

'He shall be mine,' she said. 'Do you hear me, my sisters? From now on this fisherman will serve only me.'

With that she tore off the fur hem of her long golden robe and drew it across the sleeping man's face, leaving a mark of gold upon his brow. So deep were his slumbers, however, that he did not feel a thing.

The second sister, Misty Shadow, gave a defiant laugh.

'Not so hasty, my sister,' she cried. 'Let him sleep on. When he awakes he will decide for himself.'

The third sister, Bright Sunbeam, was silent. At that moment, their father the Sun wearied of riding his boat sledge across the sky and sank down beyond the sea to rest. At once it grew dark and evening came. Off ran Bright Sunbeam to catch up with her father.

Misty Shadow meanwhile spread a soft pale-blue quilt upon the bank, stretched out her transparent arms to the fisherman, breathed a cool breeze upon him and lulled him with her vapid song. Throughout the lonely night she sang, and the fisherman's hands and feet were numbed by cold, his bones chilled and his heart frozen.

Once again, Misty Shadow laughed:

'What say you now, sister? Whom shall he serve?'

'He shall still be mine,' persisted Golden Sunshine. 'No man on earth can refuse me. Let him but gaze upon my golden form when dawn comes.'

Dawn did come, the Sun rose in the heavens and in his wake came his youngest daughter rushing to the lake; she threw back the damp quilt from the bank and caressed the fisherman with her warm bright gaze. And the longer she looked, the warmer his heart grew, fresh life spread into his frozen hands and feet. He opened his eyes and beheld a round and rosy girlish face bending over him, breathing warmth into his body. The girl was dressed in a long smock of silken strands and on her feet she wore scarlet boots.

Stretching out his arms to her, the fisherman exclaimed:

'Who are you, lovely maiden, so like the Sun's daughter?'

'But I am the Sun's daughter,' answered Bright Sunbeam.

He was much surprised at this and not a little sad.

'Why do you gaze at me so?' he asked. 'Why do you warm my heart so with your bright eyes? Would you really love a poor mortal like me and live in a dark hut?'

Without a word, she took the fisherman by the hand and they walked together along the shore until they came to his hut. After them rushed Misty Shadow dipping first to the right, then to the left, and snapping at their heels. After them, too, dashed Golden Sunshine tearing off the entire hem of her robe and scattering its golden grains upon their backs.

Yet the fisherman and the Sun's youngest daughter saw nothing as they entered the hut. So furious were the two elder sisters that they quite forgot their own quarrel and ran to the Sun to complain.

'Your youngest daughter has betrayed you, Father,' they said. 'She has wed a poor fisherman; punish her severely and make that fisherman serve us.'

In his anguish at losing his youngest, dearest daughter, the Sun wrapped himself in a storm cloud and rained his tears upon the ground. After a while, he said:

'I am very sad for Bright Sunbeam; the fate she has chosen is not a happy one. She will know some joy but much grief. Let her set aside her golden robes and forget she ever was my daughter.'

The Sun fell silent, wiped away his tears and then his fiery gaze settled on his two eldest daughters.

'As for you,' he said angrily, 'why should you be any better? You came running to tell tales. So hear my word: no longer will you run freely about the land. You, Misty Shadow, shall sit in the forest marshes guarding my underground waters; while you, Golden Sunshine, shall stand above the stone mountain guarding my underground treasures. And do not dare lay a finger on Bright Sunbeam or her husband; or I shall punish you even more severely.'

So saying the Sun enveloped himself once more in the clouds. And the sisters went their separate ways: one to the marshes by Black Varaka, the other to the top of the stone mountain. But fury at their youngest sister smouldered within them.

Meanwhile, Bright Sunbeam put aside her smock of silken strands, took off her scarlet boots, placed her sun's apparel in a chest and put on simple Saami clothing. She began to help her husband catch fish, she would dry them over a fire and cure them in the sun, she learned to make a fire and cook food, scrape reindeer hides and sew warm clothing from them. Her hands were busy all day long, yet her tender eyes always shone brightly and her round face smiled warmly. It was therefore always light and warm in the fisherman's hut even when the hearth was unlit and the Sun did not shine. And when a daughter was born to Bright Sunbeam, the hut became even brighter: so much alike were mother and daughter. So the fisherman named the little girl Akanidi after her mother.

When little Akanidi was as tall as her father's knee the fisherman said to his wife:

'In the marsh by Black Varaka there is some splendid birch bark; it will make good, stout boots. Tonight I'll go to strip the bark by the light of the moon.'

Bright Sunbeam begged him not to go, sensing some evil lurked in the dark forest swamp. Although she was now a simple Saami woman and no longer the Sun's daughter, she still knew much that ordinary folk were ignorant of. But the poor fisherman did not heed his wife's warning; he sharpened his knife, put some provisions together and, as evening drew on, set out for Black Varaka.

It was a cheerless spot, tenanted by evil spirits. The trunks of birch trees were twisted into spiral rings creeping across the ground like serpents. Truth to tell, the fisherman greatly feared the place.

He singled out a tall birch with smooth white bark inscribed with deep circles; he then took out his knife and was about to cut the bark when, to his horror, he saw an eye staring out at him, an eye of darkest blue. And out of the tree trunk came two pallid arms reaching for him. A hoarse laugh shattered the eery stillness.

'Hva, hva, hva! Ah-ha my proud fisherman, now I've got you in my clutches and you shall at last be my husband.'

Springing quickly back, he thought he must be dreaming; the eye and arms had vanished. All the same, that tree was best left alone and he started on another. But just as he put his knife to the bark, again a dark-blue eye stared out at him, pallid arms stretched to grasp his neck and a hoarse voice whispered in his ear:

'Fisherman, you will wed me.'

'Whoever you are,' he stuttered, 'let me be. I cannot marry you: I have a wife and daughter at home.'

Thereupon Misty Shadow stepped from behind the tree, her

braids of wood-smoke blue trailing upon the ground, her deep-blue eyes boring into his very soul. She waved her wispy sleeve and asked:

'Am I not comely? Have I not my own dear children – my daughter Keen-Eyes, my sons Burning Stump and Mossy Clump? You'll be father to them and feed us all.'

Hardly were the words out of her mouth than Keen-Eyes sprang on to the fisherman's chest, Burning Stump clung to his right leg and Mossy Clump to his left.

No matter how hard he tried to tear himself free, he could not move from the spot.

'How will I feed you? Where will I put you all?' the fisherman cried. 'My hut is cramped as it is.'

'Then leave your wife, I'll take her place,' said Misty Shadow. 'And you will feed me. You'll build a new hut for us all.'

Finally Misty Shadow got the better of the poor fisherman; he set to cutting down trees, lopping off their branches and putting up a new log hut. He blocked up all the cracks with mud and clay so that, as Misty Shadow ordered, the Sun should not peep in; she was much afraid of the fury of her father. When he had finished, she said:

'Now go and catch some fish for we are hungry.'

Off went the poor fisherman to his first home by the lake and told the dismal story to his wife.

'You did not heed my warning,' she said sadly. 'You went at night to Black Varaka. Now we must both serve my evil sister, Misty Shadow. There's nothing for it. Come, let us catch some fish.'

They caught some fish, cooked a whole potful and the fisherman took it to the swamp. Hardly had he entered the hut than the children set about the food, cramming their mouths full and crunching the fish bones. When the pot was empty, they cried, 'More, more!', while their mother complained that she had not even tasted any.

Once more the fisherman and his wife went fishing and cooked fish broth. Together they carried two potfuls to the hut in the swamp. The children ate their fill, then burrowed under the damp moss and went to sleep. Their mother too ate her fill before creeping into a dark corner to sleep, beckoning the fisherman to follow. She embraced him with her clammy arms and licked his face and head with her slimy tongue. As she did so, the hair began to fall from his head.

So it continued: every day the poor fisherman and his wife did the fishing, cooked two potfuls of broth and fed Misty Shadow and her young. There remained nothing to eat save mushrooms and cloudberries which their daughter Akanidi brought them from the forest. So poorly did they eat that they soon began to wither and waste away. Bright Sunbeam's lovely round face became old and wrinkled, her back bent, her bright eyes dim. The fisherman was soon a gaunt, dried-up figure with no hair on his head.

One day, up in the sky, the Sun said to his son Peivalke:

'Fly down to the lake, my son; see how Bright Sunbeam is living with her husband the fisherman.'

So Peivalke flew down to earth, circled the lake by the lakeside paths, searched among the marshes and returned to his father.

'Nowhere did I see Bright Sunbeam,' he reported. 'All I saw was an old man and woman carrying potfuls of fish broth to Black Varaka in the forest swamp. A log hut stands in that swamp; who lives there I do not know, for all the cracks and holes are blocked with slime.'

The Sun soon guessed what had happened. So he sent his son the Tempest to Black Varaka to sweep away the hut with all its mud and twigs. As her young dived deep into the mire, Misty Shadow hovered above the hummock trembling with fear.

The Sun stared at her hard, and under his fiery gaze her long braids faded away, her arms turned into toad's feet, her deep-blue eyes became puffed and dull; all that remained of her was belly and bulging head.

'Is that how you did as I ordered?' the Sun finally said. 'You are no daughter of mine; from now on you will be the old marsh witch Oadz who lives by her cunning and treachery. Let all the world see your black soul, let them fear you and let all living creatures hide from you.'

35

The Sun climbed high into the heavens, leaving ugly Oadz to sit on her hummock brooding in gloomy silence. Just then the fisherman and Bright Sunbeam came into view with their potful of broth.

'Broo, broo, broo,' croaked Oadz. 'Take pity on me, my dears.'

When the fisherman looked upon the marsh witch, he stumbled over in horror spilling the broth and dropping the pot into the swamp. At once Bright Sunbeam grabbed his hand and tugged him quickly away from Black Varaka without a backward glance.

Once again they began to live in their old home by the lake; they caught fish and brought them home, Akanidi dried their nets, kindled the fire on the hearth, cooked fish soup and helped her father and mother. She was now full-grown.

One day the fisherman came home and told his wife:

'Look, I found this golden pebble on the shore. See how it glitters.'

Bright Sunbeam looked at the pebble and recognized at once a piece of the robe of her eldest sister Golden Sunshine.

'Cast it into the deepest part of the lake,' she told her husband. 'It will bring us nothing but evil.'

She knew so very much, that wise Saami woman.

But the fisherman did not obey his wife.

'I shall certainly not throw gold back into the lake,' he said, aghast. 'Do you know what people will give for it? A whole herd of reindeer! A new net and pots! I'd best return and look for more.'

So he went back to the lakeside and searched among the sand and pebbles. And he found a few more pieces, then more and more until he had a whole potful of golden nuggets. All the while he was wandering farther and farther along the bank unable to stop himself, such was the greed that now possessed him. All day he toiled, and by evening the pieces of gold had brought him to a stone mountain that barred his path.

Instead of turning for home, he continued his search, picking out pieces of gold wherever they glittered on the mountainside. He began to strike the wall of the mountain with his knife, once, twice, three times and then, all of a sudden, the wall opened up before him. And there stood a beautiful maiden dressed in a golden robe with ruby slippers upon her feet, her green eyes sparkling like emeralds.

'I knew you would come to serve me, fisherman,' she said. 'See, my mark is still upon your brow; it took possession of your mind and guided your steps here. See how much gold I possess!'

She swept her golden arm in a wide circle showing him the golden seams in the rock, a pick and tray for washing gold, and a stream winding through the valley. In a daze the fisherman snatched up the pick and started digging at the rock. He soon filled a whole tray, washed water through it and was overjoyed to see so much gold glittering at the bottom of his pan.

Once more he took up the pick, again split the rocks, washed the pebbles and grains in his pan and piled up his store of gold. So busy was he that he did not notice the stone mountain closing, he did not see that the light of the heavens had grown dim, that dark storm clouds hung above him. Suddenly Golden Sunlight stood over his bent form, her green eyes flashing.

'Work, old man,' she commanded. 'Work on and on and do not stop.'

He needed no second bidding. The pile of gold grew higher than his head, yet still it was not enough. He raised and flung down his pick like a man possessed. But his former strength was ebbing away: his hands trembled, his legs creaked and he began to rock drunkenly on his feet. No longer did the rocks fly up from under his pick, only orange and silver sparks flew in all directions. At last he set his pick aside, his fingers numb, his spirit dead.

'What are you doing?' screamed Golden Sunshine. 'You came to serve me, so get on and serve.'

'My strength is spent,' he gasped. 'Let me rest a while and I'll recover enough strength to carry the gold away with me.'

Golden Sunshine stamped her foot so hard the sound rang all around the underground caverns.

'No one has yet taken gold from here,' she cried. 'Just look about you.'

And she made a wide sweep with her arm.

As the fisherman glanced about him, wherever his gaze settled he saw great seams of gold shining and beside them lay piles of human bones.

In the meantime, by the lake on the outside of the stone mountain, Bright Sunbeam waited two whole days for her husband. On the third she told her daughter:

'Your father did not listen to me, Akanidi. Clearly he is in trouble once more. I must go and help him. Either I shall save him or perish myself. If I do not return by tomorrow, open my wooden chest and take out my robe and boots. Cast off your walrus-hide smock and put on my silken dress; cast off your reindeer-skin stockings and put on my scarlet fur boots. Go in that attire to the top of the stone mountain and light a fire from dry grass; then take my finger and throw it into the fire.'

Thereupon Bright Sunbeam broke off the little finger of her left hand and gave it to her daughter.

'All that will remain in the fire will be a white bone. Place that bone under your left heel in the scarlet boot. Peivalke, eldest son of the Sun, will come flying down to you and ask who you are. Tell him nothing. But ask simply to be taken to his father.'

So said Bright Sunbeam, and she bade farewell to Akanidi and set off along the lakeside path towards the stone mountain.

All through the day and the night Akanidi waited for her mother, all the while straining her eyes for a glimpse of her return. But Bright Sunbeam did not come back. So at the end of the night, the girl opened the wooden chest, took out her mother's clothes and put them on. They all fitted her perfectly — the brilliant robe and the scarlet boots. Then off she went along the same path that her mother had taken toward the stone mountain. Finally, she arrived at the mountain-top and lit a fire. She placed her mother's little finger in the fire and, when all that remained was a white bone, she put it under her left heel.

In an instant, Peivalke, the Sun's first son, flew down to see who had lit a fire on the bare mountain-top. When he saw Akanidi, he was full of joy.

'Is it really you, my little sister Bright Sunbeam?' he said.

'Where have you been all this time?'

Akanidi said not a word. Then, after several moments, she asked simply:

'Take me with you when you fly to the Sun.'

'But, dear sister, have you forgotten how to fly?' he asked, surprised.

Akanidi was silent.

So Peivalke took the girl by the hand, held her tight and flew over the land straight to his father.

'See, Father,' he said, 'here is your youngest daughter, Bright Sunbeam.'

The Sun stared at Akanidi and shook his head.

'Who are you, girl?' he asked, 'so much alike to Bright Sunbeam?'

'I am Akanidi,' she replied, 'only daughter to Bright Sunbeam. My mother departed to the stone mountain to find my father and got lost. Before leaving she instructed me to put on her robe and boots and bring you all that remains of her.'

With that Akanidi removed her left boot, took the bone and handed it to the Sun. He looked fondly upon the little white bone of his dear daughter and guessed that she was no longer alive. In his great sorrow he wept and called to his children: the four Winds, the Storm Cloud twins, Lightning, Thunder and Tempest. Then the four Winds roared, the Storm Clouds darkened the sky, Thunder crashed and boomed, Tempest lashed the earth and with his fiery horns Lightning flashed and split the stone mountain in two. There stood Golden Sunshine transfixed in terror and surrounded by piles of human bones.

The Sun stared long and hard at his eldest daughter. Under his angry gaze her golden dress melted, her ruby boots became mere goat hoofs, her backbone twisted into a hump, her lovely head sank into her shoulders and her whole body grew over with black fur.

'Is that how you did as I ordered?' the Sun asked her, finally. 'You are no daughter of mine. From this day you will be the underground witch Vagahe, foul and horrid. May everyone know your black soul, may everyone fear and flee from you.'

'And you, Akanidi, will stay with me, be my Bright Sunbeam, my sweet and gentle daughter. I shall teach you to fly and to breathe life into all that lives.'

Thus spoke the Sun before riding off in his coach across the sky. After him hastened his son Peivalke and the bright maiden Akanidi. Meanwhile, Vagahe stamped her hoofs in a fury, so that the earth quaked and the mountain above her slammed shut.

When did this happen, you ask? A long time ago; so long ago that folk no longer remember. All they know is that ever since the wicked Vagahe has roamed the earth in search of her victims. Folk flee before her; for should she catch them, she would carry them off to toil inside her stone mountain.

And down in the slime of the forest swamp dwells the black-hearted witch Oadz, just as the Sun commanded. By night you may hear her sing to lead astray the passing wayfarer. Whoever draws near is seized in her toad's paws and dragged into the mud. During the day the old marsh witch hides beneath the slime afraid of the Sun, afraid of youthful Peivalke and, most of all, afraid of the brilliant gaze of the lovely Akanidi.

Should you look carefully through the branches of the trees, you may well see the pretty round face of a maid and feel the warmth of her sweet breath. That is Akanidi, the Bright Sunbeam; it is her robe that shines with its silken strands, it is her scarlet boots that sprinkle the earth with such bright berries. With her laughing eyes, she looks down upon the earth; and she loves all that lives, takes pity on all creatures and keeps them warm.

HOW HAPPINESS CAME

This is how it was.

Akanidi, Daughter to the Sun, was flying through the heavens one day and looking down upon the earth below. She warmed the reindeer in the tundra, the creatures in the forests and hills, the fish in the seas and lakes. She understood all the animals that lived and brought them happiness. Only people were beyond her comprehension: sometimes they rejoiced at her warm gaze, sometimes they scowled behind their tent flaps.

By what laws did the people live? What made them laugh? What made them cry? And why were they sometimes cruel to one another?

As Akanidi gazed down at people, she noticed that none were alike. Some ate well, dressed themselves in sable skins, yet never went hunting or kept reindeer herds. Others tended the animals for them, drove the herds to greener pastures; yet those same hard workers were ever hungry, dressed shabbily and went about with drooping heads. Akanidi felt sorry for these people and wanted to bring them happiness that would never leave them.

As evening drew nigh and the Sun completed his day's journey, he sank down beyond the sea to rest; it was then that Akanidi beseeched him:

'Let me descend to earth, Father, to the people.'

The Sun cast an angry glance at Akanidi.

'What is there on earth for you to see?' he said. 'Have you not space enough in the sky?'

'I am tired of the sky. I want to be among people,' she replied.

'But you have the clouds to play with, the sunbeams to dance with, the wind to sing songs with,' said the Sun. 'People are strange creatures; it takes little to offend them. That's how they are.'

At first Akanidi was silent. Then she pleaded again.

'Please let me go, Father, just for a short time.'

The Sun thought it over.

'All right,' he agreed, finally. 'You may fly down tomorrow. Now rest and sleep till morning.'

As soon as dawn broke, Akanidi woke up and stared about her: she was lying on a reindeer hide in a human dwelling. Before her stood an old man and woman unable to believe their eyes. They had no children and now, from out of nowhere, a young girl lay in their tent on a reindeer hide. Her face was round and rosy like a cloudberry and she stared at them warmly out of deep-blue eyes.

'Let me live in your home and be your daughter,' Akanidi said to the old folk.

The old woman was wise and had a notion what this miracle was.

'We'll gladly take you as our daughter,' she said. 'Live here as you wish.'

So Akanidi began to live with human folk and each day she ventured farther from the dwelling. But the tent stood on a tiny island in the middle of Lake Svyato under a gnarled pine tree. And not a soul lived on that island save the old couple. Akanidi now realized why her father the Sun had brought her here: he feared she would come to harm among the people.

This was not at all what she wanted; and she began to beg the old man and woman:

'Please let me go to young people, to play with them.'

But the old woman always answered:

'You are still too young even to wear a maiden's head-dress. Be patient, my girl, your time will come.'

Akanidi meantime went about her work: she helped the old woman around the tent and the old man to mend his nets, waiting patiently for her time to come. Each evening the old woman would work at the maiden's new dress which she would wear when she was full-grown. Akanidi began to stick on little stones for colors, dried fruit for gems. So lovely did it become that the old woman had never seen the like.

One day the old man made a crown from juniper twigs and the old woman dressed Akanidi in her maiden's robe, placed the crown upon her head – and Akanidi came of age. No longer was she a little girl.

Joyfully she ran down to the lake and gazed at herself in its still waters. How happy she was! She sang a merry song, danced a little dance and beamed with joy. The old man and woman gazed fondly at her and marveled at her sweet voice: it was like birds singing and the wind sighing, like leaves whispering in the trees. And their hearts became joyful.

Said the old man:

'The time has come, daughter, to take you to people. May you open their eyes and ears, Akanidi. May your heart remain full of kindness and soften the people's hearts.'

And the old woman gave Akanidi her blessing.

That night, when everyone was sleeping, a fresh breeze sprang up, bent back the old pine's branches and drove the island northwards over the lake to the mouth of a great river, the River of our Fathers. And in the morning, the old man took Akanidi over the land to meet the people. She took with her three little suede bags which she had sewn herself and decorated with dried fruits and colored stones.

They arrived at a camp, raised the flap of the nearest tent and saw a family of Saami folk sitting round the hearth eating whale meat. The fat dripped down their fingers, and their faces glistened with pleasure. That year the sea had been good to the tribe, providing them with food for many months: the waves had driven an ice mountain to the mouth of the river and in it they had found a whale frozen. The folk had cut the whale meat from the ice and each had eaten as much as he was able.

Akanidi entered the tent, and at once all the Saami folk sprang to their feet. The women wanted to caress her, to rub their cheeks against hers, the men wanted to press her tightly to their hearts, while the children wanted to play on her lap. Everyone extended a hand to her, touched her robe, caressed her braids, pulled her to them, passed her from one to the other.

Then Akanidi uttered a mysterious word: thereupon, although

she stood still, no one could touch her; their hands passed right through her as if through thin air. The women were frightened, the men puzzled, and the children began to cry. But Akanidi laughed, took a little girl by the hand, and told everyone to link hands and follow her to the river-bank. There she sang songs and danced for them.

Never had the Saami people seen or heard the like. Their eyes and ears were opened, such a great joy flooded their hearts that they took up the song and began to swirl about in Akanidi's dance.

When everyone was tired, they sank exhausted to the ground; Akanidi unnoticed took a handful of little stones and berries from her three bags and called the young girls and men to her. She pressed the palm of her hand to the ground and asked:

'Is anything there?'

'What could there be?' they said, surprised. 'Nothing is there.'

'Oh yes there is,' she exclaimed, playfully lifting her hand.

And there before them lay a beautiful pattern of circles: rings within rings, the moon and the stars, magpie feet, goose feet – and all in patterned stones that glittered in the sunshine. Then, scattering the stones and berries over the ground, she said:

'Now make patterns yourselves.'

The girls did their best, and the boys did their best, carefully piecing together little stones and berries; yet it was not as beautiful as before. Akanidi put her hand upon the ground once more, and lifted it up to reveal a fir-tree branch, reindeer antlers, the rays of the sun, waves of the sea and clouds in the sky – all multi-colored, winking and glittering in the sun.

She now handed the berries and little stones to the young women, and taught them how to adorn their boots and clothes with pretty patterns. As the days passed, they would come to show her their handiwork, and she would just touch it here and there to make the pattern even prettier. Then she would kiss the girl, rub cheeks with her and say:

'Next time you yourself will do no worse.'

The Saami girls put on their lovely new clothes and ran to look at themselves in the river. How beautiful they now were! Each tried to outmatch the other. And their boyfriends and husbands also set to decorating the maidens' boots and dresses, pleased at the beauty they were creating.

Meanwhile, Akanidi wandered from tent to tent, from camp to camp. In one place she would cut a hollow stem, make a flute from it and whistle like a bluebird or an oriole. In another she would sing a song, or tell a story, or dance a little dance. And everywhere she went she would open her little bags and give the folk the little stones and berries, teaching them to form patterns.

The Saami people began to live in happiness; joy was always in their hearts. They dressed gracefully, and sang, played and danced. Whenever they mended their nets, shepherded their herds of reindeer or journeyed in sledges, they would sing the tunes that Akanidi taught them – songs of the sun and the sea, songs of the ice mountain that had brought them whale meat, songs of good hunting fortune. And as evening drew in, they would gather in a circle and sing and dance together.

Only the elders of the tribe were not warmed by Akanidi's love. Their eyes remained closed to the beauty of her patterns, their ears shut to her stories and songs, their hearts cold to her kindness. They stared at the lovely gems she had brought and shouted:

'Bring us more.'

When Akanidi gave them more, they still cried out:

'Give us even more.'

The Sun-girl realized that it was not for joy, not for good deeds that the women wanted her gems, but to exchange them for curtains, dresses and fur boots; while the men traded them for reindeer hides, squirrel pelts and meat. The elders sat smugly in their tents growing fat from idleness, waiting for people to bring them gifts in exchange for the gems.

So Akanidi told them:

'I shall bring you no more gems.'

Thereupon they grew spiteful and cast evil glances at the girl.

'What are those songs you sing?' they shouted at the people. 'What are those dances and those patterns? The Saami folk never knew them before. When our people go hunting, when they

45

go fishing, why should they dress up and look at themselves in the rivers? We must get rid of Akanidi: she has turned our people from the ways of our fathers.'

But Akanidi could not be killed for she was protected by her father the Sun. Then it was that the elders went down to the swamp, took with them a reindeer carcass and summoned the evil old witch Oadz out of the slime to ask her help.

'Take our offering,' they said, 'only tell us how to rid ourselves of Akanidi.'

Oadz had long awaited her chance to take revenge on Akanidi, for the Saami people no longer hearkened to her melancholy songs; they now sang the happy tunes of Akanidi. No longer could Oadz entice them to her marsh. So she said to the elders:

'Take a moss-green stone, go to Akanidi in her tent and close the smoke-hole, so that the Sun cannot see her. Then kill her with the stone.'

So the evil elders found a moss-green stone, ran with it to the camp and found Akanidi sitting in her tent showing children how to make small buttons out of shells. In their haste, the elders forgot to block the smoke-hole; they threw the stone hard at Akanidi and it hit her full in the chest. But a strange thing happened: at once she faded almost clean away, sighed deeply, then sang out one last song. In the half-dark of the tent her song beat its wings against the dried walrus skins like the beating of a giant drum, and the Saami people, listening, felt their souls rise aloft, lifted by the gratitude they felt for the kind Sun-girl.

As her song came to an end, Akanidi flew up to the sky in the spiraling fire smoke.

Never again did she descend to earth. Yet her songs remained, her dances remained, and her lovely patterns remained. The Saami folk remember them, mothers pass them on to daughters, fathers to sons; and they even make up their own. It is then that their eyes and ears open, their hearts soften and happiness comes. High in the sky Akanidi gazes down on them and is happy together with them, saying to her father the Sun:

'You see, Father, what Akanidi has done.'

All that is told here is as true as the Sun's path across the heavens, as the course of time, as the change of winter to summer, day to night. This story was born in those faraway times when men and women of the Saami tribe first met Akanidi, Daughter of the Sun.

THE RAVEN AND THE OWL

In times gone by the Raven and the Owl were both as white as snow.

One day they met in the tundra and the Raven said:

'Aren't you tired of being white? I know I am. Why don't we paint each other a different color?'

'What a good idea,' the Owl replied, enthusiastically.

'Then let's begin,' said the Raven. 'You paint me first, then I'll paint you.'

'Oh no,' grumbled the Owl. 'It was you who suggested it; so you begin on me.'

'Very well,' the Raven agreed.

So he scraped some soot from a lamp, using that and a large white feather plucked from his own tail, he set about painting the Owl. With the greatest of care he daubed grey spots of every size on each feather, larger ones on the wings, smaller ones on the breast and back.

'How beautiful I've made you, Owl!' he exclaimed at last, stepping back to admire his handiwork. 'Just take a look at yourself.'

The Owl stared hard at herself and could hardly tear her gaze away.

'Yes, I really am exceedingly pretty; those grey circles are most becoming,' she admitted. 'Now let me do the same for you. By the time I finish you'll be so handsome you won't even recognize yourself.'

The Raven turned his head toward the sun, closed his eyes and stood as still as a tent pole. He was keen for the Owl to make a good job of him.

The Owl set about her work with great zeal. It took her a long time to paint the Raven to her satisfaction, but when she had, she looked him up and down with immense contentment. Yet then, glancing from the handsome Raven to herself, her expression changed: for she saw that he was now more beautiful than she was. In her envy, she quickly threw what was left of the soot all over him and flew away.

Meanwhile, the Raven rubbed his eyes and, seeing that he was now as black as black could be, he let out an angry shriek:

'You spiteful creature! What have you done to me? You've made me as black as soot, blacker than the blackest night!'

And he flapped his wings furiously as he flew off after the jealous Owl.

From that day to this, dear friends, there never was a raven that was not black from tip to tail.

HOW THE CHUKCHI PEOPLE
BECAME FRIENDS

Long ago, when the untamed mountains poured their wrath upon the valleys below, the men of the tundra were wrathful too. After one harsh feud among the tribes, a lone boy found himself left behind amid the yarangas of his people's foes. Since he was small, no one seemed to bother overmuch about him; and he was eventually taken into the home of an old man and woman.

The years passed and the boy grew into a strong and agile young man. He learned to fly on spears like a seagull, to run on the wind like a reindeer. And it was not long before the other strong and swift men of the clan came to envy him.

'Why do we harbor an enemy of our people in our midst?' they asked the elders. 'He is sure to turn his hand against us one day.'

In the end the elders pronounced their sentence: he must be slain.

However, before a life could be taken, the victim had to be provided with a good meal. Such was the custom of the tundra. So the old man told his wife:

'Prepare food, woman, such as we have never eaten before.'

The old woman understood.

She pleaded with her husband, wrung her hands and cried bitter tears. Yet he turned a stony face to all her pleas. He was no less fond of the boy than she; all the same, there was no going against the word of the elders.

When the young orphan entered the yaranga after his day with the herd, he found the old woman in tears.

'Why are you weeping, mother?' he asked. 'What is wrong?'

'Go and eat, my son,' was all she said.

50

He glanced at the meal spread before him. And he too understood.

'So be it. I shall go to meet my forefathers with no fear in my
heart.'

He ate his fill, left the yaranga and, calling his father, he said:
'Come, I am ready.'

They made their way, the old man and the youth, to a clearing
beyond the tents. And there, with trembling hand the old man
raised his bow and shot an arrow at his adopted son.

But it sped past and the young man caught it in flight. In one
swift move, he snapped the arrow in two.

A second and a third arrow also flew past. In all, a dozen
arrows were dispatched, yet not a single one found the target.
The young man caught each one in flight and broke them all.
The old man now knew he was not fated to die.

'You are not our son,' he said, at last. 'Nor are you of our
people. That is why they wish to kill you. It is clear that your
forefathers are not ready to receive you; for they will not let you
die. Go, then, and seek your own folk. Many unfriendly tents
separate you from your home. Enter none. Soon you will reach
an island in the middle of a lake. Rest there, but not for long. For
your foes will attack you. Defend yourself as best you can.
Should you survive, move on until you come to a pinewood;
climb the tallest tree and find there a raven's nest. Lie in that and
take your rest. Again, though, hostile tribes will attack you and
you must defend yourself. Should you survive again, you will
find your home among the people of the pinewoods, and there
you will be safe.'

The young man set off alone.

Along the way he encountered great camps with fine yarangas;
yet even though he was hungry and thirsty, he did not enter
them. Throughout the first day he walked until, at sundown, he
came to a big lake. And, just as the old man had said, there lay
an island in the very middle. The young man swam to it and lay
down to rest.

A fierce shout woke him at dawn and he saw several kayaks
approaching the island filled with warlike strangers brandishing

spears. As they reached the island, he flew at them as fast and destructive as a shower of spears, showing them no mercy. After a while, only three attackers remained alive.

'Go back to your people,' he said, 'and tell them that he who lives by the spear shall perish by the spear. Let them not raise their spears again.'

And he continued on his way. All through the second day he walked and walked, passing great camps with fine yarangas that beckoned to him with their warmth and promise of food. But he went on by.

The old man had not deceived him, for ahead he soon spotted thick pinewoods. Making for the tallest tree, he quickly climbed to the top and lay down to rest in a raven's nest.

At dawn he was awoken by violent shaking and, looking down, he saw a party of hunters obviously intent on killing him. Quickly snatching up his bow, he showered arrows upon the men below, showing no mercy, until only two remained alive.

'Go back to your camp,' he told them, 'and spread the word far and wide that should any person take up arms against innnocent people he will be slain.'

With that he climbed down from the tree, gathered up all the discarded spears and buried them with his own spear in a deep pit. And he carried on with his journey.

Presently he drew near a familiar encampment in a clearing of the pinewood. At the sight of the stranger, men came running from their yarangas to find out who he was. Though he told them his story and assured them he was of their tribe, his own people stared at him in disbelief, suspicious of one brought up in an enemy tent.

'Since you do not trust my word,' he said, 'I will challenge the strongest and swiftest among you to prove myself better than you.'

The young men of his own camp were eager to take up the challenge. They ran over a great distance. At first the young stranger stumbled on every stone, catching his foot against every blade of grass until he was lagging far behind the group of runners. Then, tying a little bell to his belt, he ran lightly and swiftly through the group, overtaking every one. So fast did he run that no one saw him; all they heard was the tinkling of his little bell.

When the runners at last returned to their camp, they found the young stranger waiting for them.

'Someone overtook us all,' said one, 'but we know not who it was. We did not see him, we only heard a little bell.'

At that, the young man shook his bell for all to hear and see. So now they knew who had run more swiftly than anyone! They were now prepared to follow him anywhere.

'Come with me,' he cried, 'I have a lesson to teach you.'

He led them along the path he had followed to their camp, passing through the pinewood and by the tall tree with its raven's nest. There he halted and dug up the discarded spears – all except his own. And before their astonished gaze, he broke every spear. Then he pointed to his dead enemies.

'That is what remains of those who raised their spears against me.'

They passed the lake and the island. Again he pointed to his slaughtered foes and their broken spears. On and on they went passing through many camps; yet nobody raised a spear against them.

News travels fast in the tundra.

Finally, they came to the cluster of yarangas from which the young man had started his journey.

'Wait here for me,' he told the men of his clan.

And he made straight for the tent of the old man and woman, telling them:

'No one from the clans about will take up arms: I have broken all their spears. See for yourself – no spears are left.'

Amazed, the old man went to see for himself. True enough, no one had a spear. And no one wished to make another.

'Summon the peoples together,' said the youth. 'And we shall talk in peace with no one to threaten us again.'

And so the peoples that had been enemies met and agreed to live in peace forever. Men of one clan married women of another and from that time on all the clans joined together to form one Chukchi people.

As for the young man, his work done, he settled down to live in peace with his neighbors. But he alone keeps the secret: somewhere in the pinewood by a tall tree lies his own sharp unbroken spear. It may be needed someday lest someone take up arms against the peaceful people.

THE SUN MAIDEN AND THE CRESCENT MOON

Long ago there lived a boy and girl whose parents had died when they were very small. Though life was hard they grew up strong and healthy and not a little curious about the world around them.

So when he was full-grown, the brother began to venture into the world beyond and spent several moons roaming over the open plain and noting all who lived there.

Now high up in the sky dwelt the Sun Maiden; and she, lonely creature, had no one at all to keep her company. One day she glanced down to earth and noticed a man wandering alone over the plains, looking up at the sky and wondering at her beauty.

'How I'd like to reach the Sun and traverse the heavens with her,' he sighed.

She sighed in turn:

'What a handsome young man that is; how I wish I could bring him up here. He is so far below, though, I cannot reach him.'

And the Sun Maiden began to plead with the heavens to grant her wisdom that she might think of a way to reach the young man and lift him up to her realm.

'You have long arms, Sun Maiden,' said the heavens. 'You have only to stretch them to wherever you please.'

Next morning the Sun Maiden rose and began to stretch her long slender arms toward the earth, trying to touch it. This she succeeded in doing soon enough, and at once it became warm and bright throughout the land. Seeing the young man walking below, she tried to touch him too. As she held out her hand to him, he suddenly felt her warmth and stopped.

'Why has it become so hot all of a sudden?' he wondered. 'I'd better lie down in the shade to cool off.'

And he sank to the ground in the shade of a bush. Yet the Sun Maiden would not give up. She stretched her hands closer and closer until at last she reached him and, snatching the man up swiftly, she carried him off to the skies.

The young man lived in the heavens with the Sun for a week until he could bear it no longer. All the while his thoughts were of his sister and of his former life upon the earth.

'I do not like living in the sky with you, Sun Maiden,' he said. 'I am a human and cannot dwell so high in the heavens. Let me return to earth where I belong. If you take me back, I shall visit you again. You have my word.'

Tears came to the Sun Maiden's eyes and clouded her bright face.

'You will not return, I know it,' she sobbed. 'Evil spirits will kill you and I shall be left to mourn alone.'

After a time, seeing that no words of hers could touch his heart, she yielded to him.

'Very well,' she sighed. 'I shall do as you say: I shall let you go and try to protect you from the evil spirits. Here, take this comb and whetstone to keep you safe.'

'Do not cry, Sun Maiden,' the young man said, taking her gifts. 'I shall be back, you have my promise.'

The Sun Maiden struck the heavens with her head and a winged horse appeared. Seating the man upon it, she slapped its withers and sent it flying down to earth. Presently, he found himself before his tent and was overjoyed to see his sister sitting inside.

But all was not as it seemed. For while he had been away, Hossiadam, the evil sorceress, had eaten his sister and taken her shape and countenance.

The false sister made as if to welcome him with open arms, then picking up a pot she ran down to the river for water. On her return, she hung the full pot over the fire and set to preparing a meal; while her brother rested before the fire she left the tent, stole over to the winged horse and cut off one of its hind legs.

When she returned to the tent, she threw the leg into the pot.

Brother and sister sat before the pot talking happily until suddenly the man noticed his horse's leg sticking out of it. Sensing that some evil was afoot, he looked hard at his sister and saw through her disguise: before him sat Hossiadam! Snatching up the horse's leg he dashed quickly to where his horse was tethered, knowing that if he tarried a moment longer the sorceress would kill him. But how would his horse run on three legs? It would take time to fix the fourth leg properly; nonetheless, he stuck it on as best he could, leapt on the horse's back and was off like the wind with Hossiadam in pursuit.

The horse's leg ached soon causing him to stumble and fall; in desperation the young man had to abandon the horse and take to his heels. In no time at all Hossiadam was close behind, breathing down his neck. As he looked up hopefully to the sky, he saw the Sun Maiden gazing down at him pityingly; there was nothing she could do to help him.

However, he remembered the whetstone she had given him and he quickly flung it behind him. At once a huge mountain rose up out of the ground separating him from the sorceress, who flew into a rage tearing at the stones with her claws and tossing them to all sides in her fury. She even gnawed at the mountain with her iron teeth until she had made a hole big enough to squeeze through and take up the chase again. Though he was far ahead, she was on his heels in a trice and was about to seize him when this time he flung the comb behind him. Straightaway, a dense forest sprang up blocking the path of the sorceress. Hossiadam began to gnaw at the trees, quickly felling them one after the other until she had cleared a way through the forest and could chase after the young man again. Although he was almost out of sight, he was now very tired and the sorceress was fast gaining on him, her hands stretching out to seize him.

The Sun Maiden saw that in another moment her beloved would be lost; she swiftly reached down with her slender sunrays, but she was not quick enough, for Hossiadam had seized one leg while she held the other. They began pulling at the man, the Sun Maiden trying to lift him up to the heavens, Hossiadam trying to hold him down to the ground. They pulled and strained until, in a clap of thunder, they rent the poor man in two.

The Sun Maiden found she had the half without the heart, and though she breathed all her warmth into it, she could not keep it alive for more than a short time: it would revive for a few days and then die again. And even though she put a live coal in the man's breast in place of a heart, she only managed to revive him for a week.

'I have no more power to help you,' she cried at last to the young man or, rather, to the half of him that belonged to her. 'Go to the other end of the heavens and remain there forever. From this day forth we shall be parted and see each other only on the longest day of the year; even then it will be no more than the merest glimpse.'

With these words, the Sun Maiden lifted the half-man above her head and flung him into the darkest corner of the sky where her rays could not reach. And there he remained, turning into the Crescent Moon that wanders across the dark heavens the whole year round.

Because he has no heart, his rays are cold and lifeless. So it is that the Crescent Moon and his dear Sun now see each other only on the longest day of the year.

KOTURA, LORD OF THE WINDS

In a nomad camp in the wilds of the Far North lived an old man
with his three daughters. The man was very poor. His choom
barely kept out the icy wind and driving snow. And when the
frost was keen enough to bite their naked hands and faces, the
three daughters huddled together round the fire. As they lay
down to sleep at night, their father would rake through the ashes;
and then they would shiver throughout the long cold night till
morning.

One day, in the depths of winter, a snowstorm blew up and
raged across the tundra. It whipped through the camp the first
day, then the second, and on into the third. There seemed no end
to the driving snow and fierce wind. No bold Nenets dared show
his face outside his tent and families sat fearful in their chooms,
hungry and cold, dreading that the camp would be blown clean
away.

The old man and his daughters crouched in their tent harking
to the howling of the blizzard, and the father said:

'If the storm continues for much longer, we shall all die for
certain. It was sent by Kotura, Lord of the Winds. He must be
very angry with us. There's only one way to appease him and
save the camp: we must send him a wife from our clan. You, my
eldest daughter, must go to Kotura and beg him to halt the
blizzard.'

'But how am I to go?' asked the girl, in alarm. 'I do not know
the way.'

'I shall give you a sled,' said her father. 'Turn your face into
the north wind, push the sled forward and follow wherever it
leads. The wind will tear open the strings that bind your coat; yet
you must not stop to tie them. The snow will fill your shoes; yet

you must not stop to shake it out. Continue on your way until you arrive at a steep hill; when you have climbed to the top, only then may you halt to shake the snow from your shoes and do up your coat.

'Presently, a little bird will perch on your shoulder. Do not brush him away, be kind and caress him gently. Then jump on to your sled and let it run down the other side of the hill. It will take you straight to the door of Kotura's choom. Enter and touch nothing; just sit patiently and wait until he comes. And do exactly as he tells you.'

Eldest daughter put on her coat, turned the sled into the north wind and sent it gliding along before her.

She followed on foot and after a while the strings on her coat came undone, the swirling snow squeezed into her shoes and she was very, very cold. However, she did not heed her father's words: she stopped and began to tie the strings of her coat, to shake the snow from her shoes. That done, she moved on into the face of the north wind.

On and on through the snow she went until at last she came to a steep hill. And when she finally reached the top, a little bird flew down and would have alighted on her shoulder had she not waved her hands to shoo him away. Alarmed, the bird fluttered up and circled above her three times before flying off.

Eldest daughter sat on her sled and rode down the hillside until she arrived at a giant choom. Straightaway she entered and glanced about her; and the first thing that met her gaze was a fat piece of roast venison. Being hungry from her journey, she made a fire, warmed herself and warmed the meat on the fire. Then she tore off pieces of fat from the meat; she tore off one piece and ate it, then tore off another and ate that too, and another until she had eaten her fill. Just as all the fat was eaten, she heard a noise behind her and a handsome young giant entered.

It was Kotura himself.

He gazed at eldest daughter and said in his booming voice:

'Where are you from, girl? What is your mission here?'

'My father sent me,' replied the girl, 'to be your wife.'

Kotura frowned, fell silent, then sighed.

'I've brought home some meat from hunting. Set to work and cook it for me.'

Eldest daughter did as he said, and when the meat was cooked, Kotura bade her divide it in two.

'You and I will eat one part,' he said. 'The remainder you will take to my neighbor. But heed my words well: do not go into her choom. Wait outside until the old woman emerges. Give her the meat and wait for her to return the empty dish.'

Eldest daughter took the meat and went out into the dark night. The wind was howling and the blizzard raging so wildly she could hardly see a thing before her. She struggled on a little way, then came to a halt and tossed the meat into the snow. That done, she returned to Kotura with the empty dish.

The giant looked at her keenly and said:

'Have you done as I said?'

'Certainly,' replied the girl.

'Then show me the dish, I wish to see what she gave you in return,' he said.

Eldest daughter showed him the empty dish. Kotura was silent. He ate his share of the meat hurriedly and lay down to sleep. At first light he rose, brought some untanned deer hides into the tent and said:

'While I hunt, I want you to clean these hides and make me a coat, shoes and mittens from them. I shall try them on when I get back and judge whether you are as clever with your hands as you are with your tongue.'

With those words, Kotura went off into the tundra. And eldest daughter set to work. By and by a wizened old woman covered in snow came into the tent.

'I have something in my eye, child,' she said. 'Please remove it for me.'

'I've no time. I'm too busy,' answered eldest daughter.

The old Snow Woman said nothing, turned away and left the tent. Eldest daughter was left alone. She cleaned the hides hastily and began cutting them roughly with a knife, hurrying to get her tasks done by nightfall. Indeed, she was in such a rush that she did not even try to shape the garments properly; she was intent only on finishing her work as quickly as possible.

Late that evening, the young giant, Lord of the Winds, returned.

'Are my clothes ready?' he asked at once.

'They are,' eldest daughter replied.

Kotura took the garments one by one, and ran his hands carefully over them: the hides were rough to the touch so badly were they cleaned, so poorly were they cut, so carelessly were they sewn together. And they were altogether too small for him.

At that he flew into a rage, picked up eldest daughter and flung her far, far into the dark night. She landed in a deep snowdrift and lay there unmoving until she froze to death.

And the howling of the wind became even fiercer.

Back in the Nenets camp, the old father sat in his choom and harkened to the days blown over by the northern winds. Finally, in deep despair, he said to his two remaining daughters:

'Eldest daughter did not heed my words, I fear. That is why the wind is still shrieking and roaring its anger. Kotura is in a terrible temper. You must go to him, second daughter.'

The old man made a sled, instructed the girl as he had her sister, and sent her on her way. Second daughter pointed the sled into the north wind and, giving it a push, walked along behind it. The strings of her coat came undone and the snow forced its way into her shoes. Soon she was numb with cold and, heedless of her father's warning, she shook the snow from her shoes and tied the strings of her coat sooner than she was instructed.

She came to the steep hill and climbed to the top. There, seeing the little bird fluttering towards her, she waved her hands and shooed him away. Then quickly she climbed into her sled and rode down the hillside straight to Kotura's choom. She entered the tent, made a fire, ate her fill of the roast venison and lay down to sleep.

When Kotura returned, he was surprised to find the girl asleep on his bed. The roar of his deep voice woke her at once and she explained that her father had sent her to be his wife.

Kotura frowned, fell silent, then shouted at her gruffly:

'Then why do you lie there sleeping? I am hungry, be quick and prepare some meat.'

As soon as the meat was ready, Kotura ordered second daughter to take it from the pot and cut it in half.

'You and I will eat one half,' he said. 'And you will take the other to my neighbor. But do not enter her choom: wait outside for the dish to be returned.'

Second daughter took the meat and went outside into the storm. The wind was howling so hard, the black night was so smothering that she could see and hear nothing at all. So, fearing to take another step, she tossed the meat as far as she could and returned to Kotura's tent.

'Have you given the meat to my neighbor?' he asked.

'Of course I have,' replied second daughter.

'You haven't been long,' he said. 'Show me the dish, I want to see what she gave you in return.'

Somewhat afraid, second daughter did as she was bid, and Kotura frowned as he saw the empty dish. But he said not a word and went to bed. In the morning, he brought in some untanned hides and told second daughter to make him a coat, shoes and mittens by nightfall.

'Set to work,' he said. 'This evening I shall judge your handiwork.'

With those words, Kotura went off into the wind and second daughter got down to her task. She was in a great hurry, eager to complete the job by nightfall. By and by, a wizened old woman covered in snow came into the tent.

'I've something in my eye, child,' she said. 'Pray help me take it out; I cannot manage by myself.'

'Oh, go away and don't bother me,' said the girl, crossly. 'I am too busy to leave my work.'

The Snow Woman went away without a word.

As darkness came, Kotura returned from hunting.

'Are my new clothes ready?' he asked.

'Here they are,' replied second daughter.

He tried on the garments and saw at once they were poorly cut and much too small. Flying into a rage, he flung second daughter even farther than her sister. And she too met a cold death in the snow.

Back home the old father sat in the choom with his youngest daughter, waiting in vain for the storm to abate. But the blizzard redoubled its force, and it seemed the camp would be blown away at any minute.

'My daughters did not heed my words,' the old man reflected, sadly. 'They have angered Kotura even more. Go to him, my last daughter, though it breaks my heart to part with you; but you alone can save our clan from certain doom.'

Youngest daughter left the camp, turned her face into the north wind and pushed the sled before her. The wind shrieked and seethed about her; the snowflakes powdered her red-rimmed eyes almost blinding her. Yet she staggered on through the blizzard mindful of her father's words. The strings of her coat came undone — but she did not stop to tie them. The snow forced its way into her shoes — but she did not stop to shake it out. And although her face was numb and her lungs were bursting, she did not pause for breath. Only when she had reached the hilltop did she halt to shake out the snow from her shoes and tie the strings of her coat.

Just at that moment, a little bird flew down and perched on her shoulder. Instead of chasing him away, she gently stroked his downy breast.

And when the bird flew off, she got on to her sled and glided over the snow down the hillside right to Kotura's door.

Without showing her fear, the young girl went boldly into the tent and sat down patiently waiting for the giant to appear. It was not long before the doorflap was lifted and in came the handsome young giant, Lord of the Winds.

When he set eyes on the young girl, a smile lit up his solemn face.

'Why have you come to me?' he asked.

'My father sent me to ask you to calm the storm,' she said, quietly. 'For if you do not, our people will die.'

Kotura frowned and said gruffly:

'Make up the fire and cook some meat. I am hungry and so must you be too, for I see you have touched nothing since you arrived.'

Youngest daughter prepared the meat, took it from the pot and handed it to Kotura in a dish. But he instructed her to take half to his neighbor.

Obediently, youngest daughter took the dish of meat and went outside into the snowstorm. Where was she to go? Where was the neighbor's choom to be found in this wilderness?

Then suddenly, from out of nowhere, a little bird flew before her face – that self-same bird she had caressed on the hillside. Now it flew before her, as if beckoning her on. Whichever way the bird flew, there she followed. At last she could make out a wisp of smoke spiralling upwards and mingling with the swirling snowflakes.

Youngest daughter was very relieved, and she made for the smoke thinking the choom must be there. Yet as she drew near, she saw to her surprise that the smoke was coming from a mound of snow; no choom was to be seen!

She walked round and round the mound of snow and prodded it with her foot. Straightaway a door appeared before her and an old, old woman poked her head out.

'Who are you?' she screeched. 'And why have you come here?'

'I have brought you some meat, Grannie,' youngest daughter replied. 'Kotura asked me to bring it to you.'

'Kotura, you say?' said the Snow Woman, chewing on a black pipe. 'Very well then, wait here.'

Youngest daughter waited by the strange snow-house and at last the old woman reappeared and handed her back the wooden dish. There was something in the dish but the girl could not make it out in the dark. With a word of thanks, she took the dish and returned to Kotura.

'Why were you so long?' Kotura asked. 'Did you find the Snow Woman's choom?'

'Yes, I did, but it was a long way,' she replied.

'Give me the dish that I might see what she has given you,' said the giant.

When he looked into the dish he saw that it contained two sharp knives and some bone needles and scrapers for dressing hides.

The giant chuckled.

'You have some fine gifts to keep you busy.'

At dawn Kotura rose and brought some deerskins into the choom. As before, he gave orders that new shoes, mittens and a coat were to be made by nightfall.

'Should you make them well,' he said, 'you shall be my wife.'

As soon as Kotura had gone, youngest daughter set to work. The Snow Woman's gifts indeed proved very useful: there was all she needed to make the garments.

But how could she do it in single day? That was impossible!

All the same, she dressed and scraped the skins, cut and sewed so quickly that her fingers were soon raw and bleeding.

As she was about her work, the doorflap was raised and in came the old Snow Woman.

'Help me, my child,' she said. 'There's a mote in my eye. Pray help me to take it out.'

At once youngest daughter set aside her work and soon had the mote out of the old woman's eye.

'That's better,' said the Snow Woman. 'My eye does not hurt any more. Now, child, look into my right ear and see what you can see.'

Youngest daughter looked into the old woman's right ear and gasped in surprise.

'What do you see?' the Snow Woman asked.

'I see a maid sitting in your ear,' the girl replied.

'Then, why don't you call to her? She will help you make Kotura's clothes.'

At her call, not one but four maids jumped from the Snow Woman's ear and immediately set to work. They dressed the skins, scraped them smooth, cut and sewed them into shape, and very soon the garments were all ready. Then the Snow Woman took the four maids back into her ear and left the choom.

As darkness fell, Kotura returned.

'Have you completed your tasks?' he asked.

'Yes, I have,' the girl said.

'Then show me the new clothes that I may try them on'.

Youngest daughter handed him the clothes, and Kotura passed his great hand over them: the skins were soft and supple to the touch. He put them on: the coat and the shoes and the mittens. And they were neither small nor large. They fitted him perfectly.

Kotura smiled.

'I like you, youngest daughter,' he said. 'And my mother and four sisters like you, too. You work well, and you have much courage. You braved a terrible storm so that your people might not die. And you did all that you were told. Stay with me and be my wife.'

No sooner had the words passed his lips than the storm in the tundra was stilled. No longer did the Nenets people hide from the north wind in their cold tents. They were saved. One by one they emerged into the sunshine.

And with them came the old father, tears of joy glistening on his sunken cheeks, proud that his youngest, dearest daughter had saved the people from the storm.

AIOGA

There once lived among the Samarov clan an old fisherman with a little daughter whose name was Aioga. So pretty was she that word of her matchless beauty passed round the camps and folk came from far and wide to praise her.

The little girl became extremely vain. Coyly twisting her dark tresses, she would sit and gaze at her reflection in a shiny copper pan or in the cold transparent waters of a stream. Her eyes were grave, yet when she smiled at herself a little light shone out of her eyes as if there were a candle somewhere behind.

Sad to relate, she became a lazybones who cared for no one but herself. One day her mother told her to fetch some water from the stream.

But the girl replied:

'No, I might fall into the water.'

'Then catch hold of the reeds,' said her mother.

'But the reeds might break,' answered Aioga.

'Then take hold of a strong stick,' continued her mother.

'I might scratch my hands,' said the girl.

Patiently her mother persisted:

'Wear your mittens then.'

'I don't want to tear them,' said the lazy girl, all the while staring at herself in the copper pan.

'But you may darn your mittens.'

'The needle might break.'

'Not if you use a strong one,' said her mother.

'Anyway, I might prick my finger,' the girl said.

Listening to these words, the neighbor's daughter told Aioga's mother:

'I'll go for the water if you like, Mistress.'

And off she ran.

Meanwhile, Aioga's mother mixed some dough and made a plate of scones, baking them on the fire's embers. When Aioga saw the scones, she cried:

'Give me a scone, Mother.'

'They are still hot,' her mother replied. 'You'll burn your fingers.'

'Then I'll put on my mittens to eat it.'

'But your mittens will get soiled,' said her mother.

'I'll wash them in the stream.'

'But they'll shrink,' replied her mother.

'Don't worry, I'll stretch them again.'

At that her mother thought to teach her a lesson.

'Why should you work and spoil your delicate skin? Even should you eat a scone, you would surely scald your mouth or roughen your hands. Better for me to give it to our neighbor's girl who doesn't mind spoiling her hands.'

So Aioga's mother gave a scone to the neighbor's daughter.

Aioga flew into a temper, stamped her foot and ran off to the river to gaze at her reflection in the water. On the bank sat the neighbor's girl quietly munching the scone. When Aioga saw her, she stared a very angry stare at her.

And a strange thing happened.

Her neck began to grow. It grew and grew until it was quite two arm-lengths long.

Said the neighbor's daughter in alarm:

'Please take the scone, Aioga, I'm not hungry really.'

Aioga grew even more angry, waved her arms above the girl so violently that her fingers became as white and fluffy as the wind-blown snow. All of a sudden she sprouted feathers as her arms turned into wings.

'I want nothing, no-oh-oh-oh!' she cried.

With that cry on her pale lips, she toppled over the bank, slid into the water and turned into a swan.

As she swam round and round, she repeated over and over again:

'Oh, how pretty I am. Oh, Oh, Oh, how pretty I am!'

She swam and swam until she quite forgot the Nanai tongue. All and every word.

Only her name remained so that no one would confuse her with other lovely creatures. Thus, she cried for all to hear and envy:

'Ai-oga-ga-ga! Ai-oga-ga-ga! Ai-oga-ga-ga!'

BRAVE AZMUN

The deeds of the brave are spoken of down the years: a father
tells his son, and the son passes it on to his son. So it is with this
tale. It began long ago when Nivkhs went fishing with wooden
hooks, when their arrows were tipped with wood, and when the
Amur estuary was known as Lya-eri, the Little Sea, and the
island of Sakhalin known as the Tro-Miff.

And in those far-off times, there stood a Nivkh camp on the
banks of the River Amur. When fish were plentiful, the Nivkh
folk made merry, sang songs and filled their bellies to the brim.
But when fish were scarce, the Nivkh fell silent, smoked moss
and sat starving in their tents.

One spring, in those long-forgotten days, our Nivkh kinsmen
were sitting on the Amur's banks, gazing at the water, smoking
pipes and mending nets, when some floating logs came into sight.
It was a clump of five or six, or perhaps a dozen trees. Evidently a
storm had blown them down, flood water had swept them
together and they were now stuck so fast that nothing could
separate them. Soil had blown on to the logs and with it seeds of
grass so there was grass now growing on them: a whole island
was floating down the river.

And in the middle of the island stood a wooden pole with a red
rag tied on top. There were several rows of notches cut into the
pole, through which the wind whistled.

An old Nivkh, Pletun, spoke up:

'Someone must be on that floating island; they've stuck in the
pole and rag to ward off evil spirits.'

And then, as the people strained their ears, they could just
make out a child crying somewhere on the island.

'That child seems to be alone,' said Pletun. 'It could be that enemies have slain his kin or the black death has carried them off; maybe his mother sent him downriver in the hope that he would be found.'

As the island came closer, the people on the bank could hear the cries of a young child more clearly. Men prepared a hooked line, threw it on to the logs and pulled them to the bank. And then they saw the child lying in a cradle: he was pale and round with black eyes that glittered like little stars, and with a face as wide as the full moon. In his hands he was holding an arrow and an oar.

As soon as Pletun saw this, he pronounced that the child would be bold and brave and would fear neither work nor any foe.

'I shall make him my son,' said old Pletun, 'and he shall bear the name Azmun.'

The Nivkhs took Azmun in their arms and carried him to Pletun's tent. Yet as they walked, the child seemed to grow heavier with every step.

'Hey, Pletun,' they called, 'your son is growing before our eyes.'

'Well, he's sure to grow fast in friendly arms on friendly soil,' answered the old man.

So big was Azmun by the time they reached the tent that he slid from their arms and stood on his feet, letting the older people enter first before he went in himself.

'The lad thinks of others before himself,' murmured Pletun, approvingly.

Azmun waited until his new father was sitting on the plank bed, then bowed to him and said:

'Sit down, Father. You are weary from your long years. Rest awhile.'

Taking up some fishing nets and oars, the lad went down to the river and launched a small boat into the water. Then, standing up in the boat, he cast his oar into the middle of the river: and the oar began to do its work, stirring up the water and stunning the fish. Azmun then dropped his net into the water and brought a teeming netful of fish into the boat. He took them back to the camp and distributed them among the Nivkh women. The Nivkh folk ate well that day, but Azmun was sad.

'There are few fish in this part of the river,' he told his father.

'It is many moons since we have had a good store of fish in the Amur,' said Pletun.

'Then we shall have to go and ask for them,' the boy said. 'How can the Nivkhs live without fish?'

In days gone by, the Nivkhs always asked the river for fish; they even fed it so that it would grant them a good catch. And so it was that now the Nivkhs went down to the river to make their supplications. In a great shoal of little canoes, dressed in their best sealskin and black-dog furs, they crowded in the centre of the river singing their songs of praise.

Pletun threw upon the waters his best dried fish, dog meat and a pinch of tobacco; all of his gifts disappeared into the Amur.

'We simple folk beg you to send us fish,' he cried, 'a whole lot of fish, all kinds of fish. We offer you dried fish and dog meat – it is all we have, for we are near starvation. Our stomachs are so empty they cling to our spines. Help us and we shall not forget you.'

Azmun cast his net into the water and pulled out a good catch once more. The Nivkhs were overjoyed, but Azmun frowned. And when he pulled up his net a second time, sure enough, the catch was less. Again he frowned. A third time he cast his net into the Amur, and brought out the last of the fish. Thereafter, whoever cast his net upon the water caught nothing at all. Not even a tiny smelt. When Azmun cast his net a fourth time, it came up empty.

The Nivkhs despaired. They sat and sucked on their pipes, muttering resignedly:

'We must die now. It is so willed.'

Azmun instructed them to store all the fish in a barn so that the people could be fed a little at a time. That done, he and Pletun sat alone by their tent, tired and hungry.

'I made you my son', said Pletun, 'thinking I would give you a new life. But now there's no fish, what shall we eat? We shall all die of starvation. Go away, my son. Leave us to our misfortune.'

Azmun was lost in thought; he smoked his father's pipe so long the smoke filled three whole barns. He thought for a long time before speaking:

'Then I must go to Tairnads, the Old Man of the Sea. I shall ask him why there are no fish in the Amur, why he has forsaken the Nivkhs.'

Pletun was afraid: no one from among the Nivkhs had ever dared to visit the Old Man of the Sea. Could an ordinary mortal descend into the depths to visit Tairnads?

'Do you have strength for the journey?' his father asked.

Azmun stamped his foot upon the ground and at once he sank up to his waist. That's how strong he was! He punched a boulder with his fist and at once the boulder cracked open and water trickled out. Screwing up his eyes, he peered into the distance towards a far-off hill.

'At the foot of that hill,' he said, 'sits a squirrel holding nut in its teeth which it cannot crack. I shall help it.'

Taking his bow, he fitted an arrow to it, pulled back the string and let fly. The arrow flew straight and true, struck the nut in the squirrel's mouth and broke it in two without harming the little creature.

'There, now you have proof of my strength,' exclaimed Azmun.

And he began preparing for the journey. First he placed some Amur soil in a sack tied to his waist, some colored beads, then a knife, his bow and arrows, a string with a hook on the end, and a mouth harp – to play should he be bored on the way.

Promising to send his father news, he went on his way. He journeyed all the way to the Little Sea and there he saw a seal winking an eye at him.

'Hello there, friend,' he cried. 'Is it far to the Master?'

'Of which master do you speak?' the seal asked.

'Tairnads, the Old Man of the Sea.'

'Then you had better look for him in the sea,' the seal replied.

On he went until he came to the Okhotsk Sea, to Pilyakerkha as it was known then. And before him stretched the open sea, so vast its boundaries could not be seen. Seagulls flew overhead, cormorants screeched, the waves chased one another on to the shore, and a gray sky hung above the sea. Where would he seek the Master in this gray wilderness? There was nobody save the birds to ask.

'Hello there, friends,' he called to the seagulls. 'Is the catch good?'

'Awful!' squawked the seagulls. 'See for yourself, we can hardly flutter our wings. We haven't seen a fish for ages: soon all our people will die. It seems the Old Man has fallen asleep and forgotten about us.'

'I am on my way to him now,' said Azmun. 'Though, truth to tell, friends, I do not know the way.'

'There is an island far out to sea that gives forth smoke,' said the seagulls. 'It isn't really an island at all, it is the roof of Tairnad's yurta, and the smoke comes from his chimney. We haven't been there ourselves, but we've heard the story from migrating birds.'

Azmun went down to the sea's edge and walked far along the shore. At last, feeling weary, he sat down on the sand, his back against a rock, and put his head in his hands and fell asleep.

Through his dreams he seemed to hear people talking and playing on the shore. As he opened his eyes, he saw young men running along the sand playing leap-frog and having playful sword-fights. While they were frolicking a band of seals came to the shore and the young men immediately set about them with their swords, killing them all.

'I'd like to have a sword like that,' thought Azmun.

While the young men were dividing up the seal meat, they left their sabers on the sand, and nobody noticed as Azmun swung his line and hooked one, pulling it to him.

When the young men had finished with the seals, they each took up their sabers from the sand; of course one was missing. A young man cried out:

'Oy-ya-ya! What is the Master going to say when he learns of my loss?'

'Ah-ha,' thought Azmun. 'That lad knows the Master. These men are evidently from the island I am seeking.'

So he lay there watching, as the men searched for the missing saber. After a time, they went down to the shore; their sabers turned into boats and they rowed out to sea, leaving the lone searcher on the shore. In haste, as the abandoned young man disappeared into the trees, Azmun dipped his saber into the water. At once it became a boat, and he jumped in and rowed after the other craft. By now they were far out to sea and although he plied his paddle as fast as he could, the other boats were soon out of sight.

What was he to do now?

There were no boats, and no young men to be seen. All he could see was a school of little whales swimming before him, their erect back-fins piercing the waves like sabers: and on each fin was a piece of seal meat.

As he gazed at the whales, Azmun felt his boat rocking under him. Holding on tight, he glanced down and saw he was riding on the back of a little whale.

Of course!

It had not been young men playing on the shore at all, but little whales. It had not been swords they were playing with, but the back-fins of whales. He was not afraid.

'All the better,' he thought. 'I shall arrive at the Old Man's island even quicker.'

However, so long did the journey take that Azmun grew a beard along the way. After many, many moons, he finally saw an island ahead looking like the roof of a giant yurta. And on the island's summit was a hole from which smoke was curling. As Azmun's whale was drawing near to the island, it suddenly rolled over on to its back, throwing Azmun into the cold sea; it was obviously afraid to face the Master without its saber. While Azmun swam in the water, the other little whales reached the island and at once turned back into young men holding the seal meat in their hands.

As soon as they saw Azmun thrashing about in the sea, they swam toward him and brought him ashore. Looking hard at him and frowning, they asked:

'Who are you? How did you get here?'

'Do you not recognize your own flesh and blood?' said Azmun. 'I fell behind you when looking for my saber. Here it is, now I've found it.'

'True enough, that is your saber,' they replied. 'But why are you so unlike yourself?'

'I was so scared when I lost my sword,' said Azmun, 'that I still haven't come to myself. Perhaps if I go to the Master he will return me to my proper form.'

'The Old Man is sleeping,' the men replied. 'You can see his smoke still curling.'

And off the men went, each to his own yurta, while Azmun remained on the shore alone. He began to climb the hill and was half-way up when he came upon a little camp on the hill-side, with nothing but girls there. And they now blocked his path.

'The Old Man is sleeping,' they said, crossly. 'Nobody must disturb him.'

But then they began to whisper sweet words to Azmun and to caress him.

'Do not go to Tairnads, stay with us. Choose yourself a wife and you will live well here.'

The girls were indeed extremely beautiful, each fairer than the next: they had pretty pale faces, lithe bodies and skillful hands. One such lovely maiden could certainly make Azmun a good wife.

Such were his thoughts when, in the pouch round his waist, the Amur soil began to stir reminding him that he had not come for a bride. Yet he still could not tear himself away from the lovely girls; so he took some beads from his pouch and scattered them over the ground.

At once the girls ran to pick them up: and as he tore his gaze from them, Azmun saw for the first time that instead of legs the girls had flippers.

They were not girls at all, but seals!

While the seal-girls were gathering up the beads, he passed by quickly and climbed to the top of the hill. Hooking the end of his line on to a spur, he dropped the line through the hole in the hilltop and climbed down into the home of the Old Man of the

Sea. As he dropped to the floor, he looked about him and was surprised to see that the Master's yurta was just like that of any Nivkh: there were the plank bed, hearth, walls, tent pole – but all were covered in fish scales. What is more, through the window he could see only water instead of sky. As he looked out he saw green waves glistening and sea plants bobbing in the waves like slender trees. Past the window swam such fish that no Nivkh would ever taste: great spiny monsters with long rows of sharp teeth.

Before Azmun, on the plank bed, lay the Master sound asleep, his wavy grey hair spread over his pillow. From the corner of his mouth jutted a pipe, a thin line of smoke curling upwards from it through the chimney. So loudly did he snore that no other sound could be heard. And when Azmun shook him by the shoulder, he did not stir.

It was then that Azmun remembered his mouth harp, his kungakei; he took it out of his pouch, fitted it between his teeth, drew it tight with his tongue and began to play: the kungakei hummed and twanged and gave out music as if a bird was chirping, as if a brook was gurgling, as if a bee was buzzing.

Tairnads had never heard the like. He stirred, sat up, rubbed his eyes and set his feet down upon the floor. Tairnads was a giant: he towered over Azmun like a cliff above the sands. His skin was covered in mother-of-pearl scales and his attire was sewn from sea plants; his wrinkled old face with its catfish whiskers was nonetheless quite kindly.

Seeing the tiny fellow standing before him like a smelt before a sturgeon, and holding the mouth harp that gave out such sweet music, Tairnad's sleep vanished from him and his warm heart pounded fast.

'Of what clan are you, young fellow?' he asked.

'I am Azmun from the Nivkhs.'

'But the Nivkhs dwell on the Tro-Miff and the Lya-eri,' said Tairnads. 'Why have you come so far to my land beneath the sea?'

Azmun told the Old Man about the troubles that had befallen the Nivkhs. With a bow, he urged:

78

'Tairnads, help the Nivkhs, send them fish. They are dying of hunger.'

Tairnads blushed in his shame.

'Yes, it's a bad business,' he murmured. 'I just sat down to take a rest and went off to sleep. I'm grateful to you for rousing me.'

With that he thrust his hand under the bed and brought out a great chan in which swam all manner of fish: humpbacked salmon, trout, kaluga and sturgeon. Fish big and small.

Next to the chan lay a whale skin; now the Old Man picked it up and filled it a quarter full with fish. Opening the door, he threw the fish into the sea, shouting:

'Swim to the Nivkhs on Tro-Miff and up the Amur, swim, swim as fast as you can, so that you can be caught in the spring.'

'Tairnads,' said Azmun, 'pray do not begrudge the Nivkhs your fish. Give them more.'

Poor Azmun was afraid he had been too bold, for he could see Tairnads was very cross. But, remembering old Pletun, he looked the Old Man straight in the eye.

At last Tairnad's scowl softened to a smile.

'I would not permit any other to talk so,' he said. 'But I pardon you, for I see that you think of others and not yourself. Let it be as you say.'

And he cast another half-skinful of fish into the sea.

'There, swim up the Amur to the Nivkhs, make their autumn catch a joyful one.'

Azmun bowed before him.

'Tairnads, I am a poor man,' he said. 'I have nothing to repay your kindness with. Nothing except my kungakei.'

So he handed Tairnads his mouth harp and showed him how to play it. The Old Man was pleased with the gift. He placed it in his mouth, clenched his teeth and began to make it sing with the tip of his tongue.

The kungakei hummed and buzzed: at first like a sobbing sea breeze, next like a wailing wind, then like the rustling of the trees, a full-throated bird at a sunrise and, last of all, like a gopher whistling shrilly at sundown. Tairnads played on merrily:

he walked through his yurta, dancing and prancing so hard the waves surged against the windows and the sea plants tore free from their moorings. A storm raged across the sea.

Azmun saw that Tairnads no longer noticed him, so he climbed back up the chimney and out into the sunlight. But his hands were soon chafed by the molluscs and barnacles that had formed on his line while he was in the Master's yurta.

When he looked about him from the hilltop he saw the seal-girls were still searching for the beads, bickering as they shared them out; they had clearly forgotten all about their homes, for the tent flaps were now overgrown with moss and lichen.

Azmun looked farther on to the lower village and saw that it was now deserted; he could just make out the little whales far out to sea, chasing fish towards the shores of Pilya-kerkha and down the Amur. But how was he to get home?

And then he noticed a rainbow hanging in the sky, one end on the island, the other on the Great Land. All about him the waves were tumbling over the sea and white horses tossed their manes as Tairnads danced on in his yurta. Azmun took hold of the rainbow and began climbing up; it was very slippery and the colors came off on him. Before long Azmun's face was green, his hands were yellow, his stomach red and his legs blue. Somehow he pulled himself to the top of the rainbow, then slipped all the way down the other side to the Great Land. On the way, as he looked down, he could see the waters below simply black with fish. The Nivkhs would certainly never lack for fish again.

As he landed on the ground, he saw the poor whale-boy sitting on the seashore; at once he handed him back his sword.

'Oh, thank you,' said the whale-boy. 'I was sure I would never see my home again. For your kindness I shall drive the fish all the way up the Amur to the Nivkh camp.'

With that he rolled over on to his back and turned into a little whale, his sword now his back-fin sticking up through the water as he swam out to sea.

Azmun walked on toward the Great Sea and there came upon the seagulls and cormorants.

'Hello, friend,' they squawked. 'Did you find the Old Man?'

'Yes,' Azmun called back. 'Just look down at the sea.'

There were so many fish that the waters simply teemed with them. Down dived the hungry birds after them and became fat before Azmun's eyes.

On went Azmun until he had passed the Lya-eri and was approaching the Amur. Suddenly he came upon the young seal lying exhausted upon the shore.

'Did you find Tairnads?' it whispered, hoarsely.

'Yes, I did,' the boy said. 'Just look in the Lya-eri.'

So thick with fish were the waters of the Lya-eri that they frothed and foamed; and the little seal slid into the sea to catch some. As it caught and ate them, it grew fatter with every minute.

On and on went Azmun until he finally arrived at the Nivkh camp. There were the Nivkhs still sitting on the shore, but now more dead than alive; they had smoked the last moss and eaten the last fish. Old Pletun came out of his yurta to greet his son, inhaling the odor of his face and neck and kissing him on both cheeks.

'Did you reach the Old Man, my son?' he asked.

'Look not at me, Father,' the boy exclaimed. 'Just gaze into the Amur!'

The waters of the Amur were seething with fish of every kind. When Azmun hurled his harpoon into the river, he speared a dozen fish at once – that many were there.

'Is that sufficient fish, my father?' he asked.

'It is,' the old man replied, with a smile.

From then on the Nivkhs had plenty of fish in spring and autumn, summer and winter.

Many heroes of those far-off days are now forgotten. But the memory of Azmun and his kungakei has never dimmed. When the sea is restless and waves lash the barren cliffs, Nivkhs can hear the grey crests hiss above the waves, the birds whisper in the breeze, the gophers whistle on the plain and the trees rustle in the forest. They know it is really Tairnads, the Old Man of the Sea, playing on his kungakei and dancing in his underwater yurta to keep himself awake.

WHY HARES HAVE LONG EARS

When the animals first appeared in the forest, the Great Elk was the most fearsome among them. One time it happened as the Great Elk and his wife were taking a stroll that a Hare chanced by and overheard them talking; he crept closer and hid behind a tree stump that he might hear them better.

'I have a set of old antlers,' the Great Elk was saying, 'which I want to give away. But I really don't know who should have them.'

Thought the little Hare to himself:

'I could do with a set of big horns. I could frighten all the other animals with them.'

And he was about to shout out his claim when the Elk-Wife said:

'Give one to the Reindeer; he is our closest relation.'

'Then that's settled,' said the Elk. 'But who should have the other one?'

Before the Elk-Wife could reply, the Hare hopped out from behind the stump and called out:

'Me, me, Great Elk! Give it to me!'

'You?' exclaimed the Elk in astonishment. 'Come now, Brother, what would you want with my antlers?'

'I would scare away all my enemies,' said the Hare, boldly. 'Everyone would walk in fear of me.'

'Then so be it,' said the Elk. 'Take them, by all means.'

How delighted the Hare was: he skipped and jigged around the clearing until – plop! – a little cone fell from a cedar right on his head.

Poor Hare almost jumped out of his skin. He rushed off like the wind, tangling his new horns in bushes and shrubs until he was soon stuck fast.

Meanwhile, the Elk and his wife laughed and laughed at the Hare's silly antics.

'No, no, Brother,' called the Great Elk. 'You are too timid to wear my antlers; they cannot help you. Henceforth you shall have long ears: let all the world know how inquisitive you are!'

And that is how the Hare came to have such long ears.

THE BOY AND THE TIGER

Our story had its source in times long past.

Whenever a father went hunting he used to take his young son with him, and the boy would help his father by cutting wood and boiling tea. However, one night as he lay beside his camp fire, the father had a dream in which a tiger told him:

'Leave your son to me. If you do not, I shall not let you return home alive.'

The old hunter rose while his son still slept, wondering what he should do. If he did not give up his son, the tiger would eat them both. How could he save his life yet abandon his son to the tiger? And there was his wife and family to think of. In the end, he decided sorrowfully to go home alone, leaving his son behind.

'If the tiger eats him, I'll return and gather up his bones,' he said, resignedly.

With these gloomy thoughts, he left his slumbering son in the clearing by the camp fire.

When the boy had slept away his weariness, he rose and was surprised to find his father missing.

'No doubt he's gone off hunting,' he thought.

But as he peered into the trees he saw two great yellow eyes staring at him: it was the fearsome tiger. In great fright, he quickly climbed to the top of a tree with the tiger close behind; the boy could feel the beast's hot breath on his bare feet. But then, as fortune would have it, the tiger became stuck between two branches and could not move up or down.

The boy nimbly sprang into the branches of a nearby tree and quickly scrambled down to the ground; there he calmly drank some tea, cooked a breakfast for his father and sat down to await his father's return.

Evening came but still there was no sign of his father. The boy finally tired of waiting and lay down to rest. In his dreams he saw the tiger begging to be rescued and promising him all manner of rewards.

Next morning the boy took an axe and cut down the tree in which the tiger was stuck; he chopped and hacked at the tree until it toppled over. Unharmed, the tiger freed himself, roared his thanks and quietly moved away into the trees.

That night the boy had another dream in which the tiger came to him and said:

'Get up early in the morning and set your traps; draw a circle round them with your sleeve.'

The boy did as he had dreamed, and on the following day he went to see what he had caught: he was delighted to find that every trap contained a sable. In such manner he assembled a great pile of sables day after day.

In the meantime, his father lingered in the settlement not daring to return to seek his son's remains. But it had to be done, so eventually he set off for the hunting tent in the middle of the forest. How amazed he was to see smoke curling from the smoke-hole: his son was alive and well!

The old man found his son sitting in the tent surrounded by a great pile of rich sable; how happy the two were to see each other again. They quickly loaded up the sledge and returned home, never again to be parted in the forest.

THE CUCKOO

There was once a woman with four children who would never obey her. From dawn to dusk they tumbled and rolled in the snow until, at the end of the day, their clothes were wet and torn. Of course, their poor mother had to dry and mend them. And when they trod snow into the tent, she had to sweep it out.

The mother did the fishing, the cooking, the cleaning and the curing of skins with no help from anyone. Her life was full of suffering and one day she fell ill. As she lay in her bed, she called her children to her:

'My children, obey your mother this once, I beg of you. My throat is so dry, bring me water from the stream.'

The unhappy woman waited on her bed. But no one answered her call. It was not until evening that the children, hungry and tired, entered the tent and were surprised to find their mother struggling to put on her old gray cloak. How astonished they were to see the cloak suddenly become covered in gray feathers. And then, as she reached up to take her hide-curing board, it turned into a bird's tail. Her leather thimble became a beak and her arms turned into wings.

The poor woman had turned into a bird.

'Look, look, Mother is flying away,' shouted the eldest child, as the bird flew out of the tent and up into the sky.

The four children rushed after her, crying:

'Mother, Mother, come back, we'll bring you water!'

But on the wind came back a call:

'Cuc-koo, Cuc-koo, Cuc-koo. Too late, too late, too late.'

For full two moons the children ran after their mother, stumbling over rocks and tufts of grass, following the curves of the land that led across the tundra. Soon their bare feet were torn and bleeding so that they left a crimson trail wherever they ran.

But the mother had abandoned her family for good.

Since that time, the cuckoo has never built a nest, nor raised her own children. And red moss is sprinkled like drops of blood across the barren tundra.

HOW ANGA FETCHED A SERPENT'S SKIN AND A BEAR'S FUR

My story had its start a long, long time ago when the earth was young. Much time has passed. Where streams coursed, tall mountains now stand; where bare mountains stood, broad streams now run.

And in those days long ago there lived a Nanai woman Vaida with her young son Anga. No man dwelt in their tent, for Anga's father had been eaten by a tiger when the son was a baby.

One day Vaida fell sick and lay on her bed unable to rise. When the neighbors came, they exclaimed:

'It is the work of the boosiyoo; the evil spirits have entered Vaida's body and are tormenting her. We must find a way to drive them out before it is too late.'

The clan gathered in Vaida's tent, blew out the lamp and raised their voices to scare out the boosiyoo. In the darkness of the tent they banged on iron pots, rattled sticks, wailed and shrieked:

'Haaa-haa-yahh! Haaa-haa-yahh!'

But nothing helped the sick woman.

So at last they summoned a shaman. And he arrived in his shaman dress and horned hat, warmed his tambourine over the burning embers, then shook it hard. He banged it in an increasing rhythm, himself swirling in the full firelight of the tent, his sacred robes twirling, his lips flecked with foam. After a time, his soul departed on the sound of the drum to the mountain-top in the western heavens where there is no day but continual night, where there is always mist and the moon is but a thin crescent.

And there he communed with the spirits.

Some time later his soul returned and the shaman uttered his pronouncement. His words sent shivers through the clan.

'Vaida will die,' he said, 'unless someone can bring her the skin of the serpent Ogloma and the fur of the Great Bear. To find Ogloma he must cross the icy tundra; yet there another danger lies in wait, for near Ogloma dwells an even fiercer serpent, Simoon. And she is so fearsome that she slays anyone who dares approach her. Simoon breathes such fire as would burn off a man's arm in an instant'.

The tent was silent. All the while young Anga listened, took in the shaman's words and kept his peace.

The shaman continued:

'There is no one who would dare approach the land of the Great Bear. He lives in a cavern deep in the heart of a towering mountain that is too steep to climb. Where would we find such a bold warrior to go in search of these terrible monsters?'

The old women shook their heads and went their ways, leaving the sick mother and her son alone in the tent. From her bed Vaida gazed mournfully at her son, tears of pain and grief rolling down her pallid cheeks.

'So I shall die on this bed . . . How will you then live, my poor son?'

'Dry your tears, mother,' Anga replied. 'I shall save you: I shall fetch the serpent's skin and the bear's fur, never fear!'

'Oh no,' his mother groaned. 'You are too small for such a deed. You would perish, little Anga.'

'I do not fear those tasks,' Anga answered bravely. 'Now I must get ready for the journey.'

He set to sharpening his spear, took a large pot, slung a long leather thong over his shoulder, and set off. Along the way he scraped resin from the pines and put it in his pot.

His journey was long and wearying and on the fifth day he came to a stream. By the side of the stream grew an enormous tree, broader and taller than all the trees around. So tall was it that its foliage blocked out the sun in the daytime and the moon at night. And all around the tree lay parched and withered land.

'This must be the tree beneath which the serpent Simoon lives,' Anga thought to himself.

So he set to scraping moss from the stones and when he had a lot, he covered his body in moss, tying it on as tightly as he could with the leather thongs. That done, he waded into the stream and lay down in the shallow water, allowing the moss to soak. Then he climbed out on to the bank and banged his spear upon his iron pot as loudly as he could. Such a terrific din was raised that all the birds flew off and the wild beasts scattered to the four winds.

The serpent Simoon heard the noise and slithered out from her tent; closer and closer she came toward Anga, hissing as she did so; behind her she left a red trail of fire over the stones and grass.

Simoon came up to Anga, opened wide her jaws and sent a jagged flame at him; but the wet moss protected him from the fire. The serpent sent more fierce tongues of fire that burned every living thing to ash around the boy; but Anga remained untouched, a cloud of steam rising above him. When the serpent paused, he quickly took up his potful of pine resin and hurled it into her gaping jaws. The resin melted and ran down Simoon's throat into her belly; and soon she was dead.

At that moment, a second serpent appeared and said to Anga:

'I am the serpent Ogloma. All my life I have feared Simoon and could never overcome her. She devoured all my children, one after the other. Now you have rid me of her. Tell me: what may I give you in reward?'

'I wish for one thing only,' answered Anga. 'Give me one of the skins from your body so that I may cure my mother.'

Ogloma willingly gave Anga one of her skins, and he went on farther.

He walked on and finally came to a towering mountain; so high was it that just to gaze up at its summit would make your hat fall off. Undaunted, Anga began to climb the mountain. Clutching each sharp outcrop, he moved upward slowly and painfully; his hands were soon torn and bleeding. Yet he paid no heed, thinking all the while of his mother lying sick upon her bed.

At last, he came to a ledge which was the entrance to a deep cavern. As he walked down the tunnel to the cavern he came upon a bear of enormous size – the lord of all bears – the Great

Bear himself. He lay in a corner fast asleep, paws spread awkwardly above his head, moaning in his fretful slumber.

Looking down at him, Anga noticed a sharp splinter buried deep in one of his paws. And suddenly Anga felt pity for the bear: tying his rope round the big splinter, he began to pull with all his might and, with a final hard tug, he extracted the splinter from the bear's paw.

At once the Great Bear awoke with a growl of pain. At the sight of Anga holding the splinter, he spoke his thanks:

'For three long years I have suffered. No matter what I did I was never able to pull out that splinter. And now my torment is at an end. You have saved me. What can I give you, just tell me?'

'Give me your fur,' said Anga, 'that I may cure my mother.'

The Great Bear took off his fur and handed it to Anga, who set off at once back to his settlement. Like a young buck, he rushed headlong down the mountain and through the forest to join his people. Before long he reached his tent and presented his mother with the skin of the serpent Ogloma and the fur of the Great Bear.

She pressed the skin and the fur to her aching parts and straightaway all the pain drained from her. From that time on the Nanai clan has sung of the valor of bold young Anga.

THE SILVER MAID

In a Saami village there lived a maid who was fleet of foot. Many were the youths who came to court her, but she would run away from them into the forest. And none could catch her.

Now in the village dwelt a young man who was certain he could catch the fleet-footed maid. And he made up his mind to marry her.

When he called at her home, the maid, of course, raced off into the forest. At once the young man took up the chase. So sure was the maid that he could not catch her that she would stop now and then to tease him; and then she would dash off again.

The chase continued through the forest and over the plain until at last, seeing that the maid was harder to catch than he had reckoned, the young man tried to tire her out by forcing her up a hill. Higher and higher they went until, with the youth hard on her heels, the maid reached the top and leapt high into the air . . . and vanished into a dark cloud.

By now the young man's strength was spent and, seeing nothing but the bare hilltop, he sank to the ground exhausted, like a stricken stag. When she saw him lying senseless upon the ground, the maid at once descended from her cloud and bent over him. Her fear turned to pity.

'Is there anything I can bring you?' she asked.

'Water,' gasped the young man.

No water was to be found upon the hill; but eager to revive the handsome youth, the maid tried to squeeze some milk from her own breast and let the drops fall between his lips. This was not easy to do: he lay motionless upon the earth and the wind was blowing hard upon the hilltop. In no time at all the wind had spread the milk across the sky, so forming what folk call now the

Milky Way. Some of the milk spilled over the maid herself turning her into a solid block of silver.

Henceforth she was known as the Silver Maid.

The young man meanwhile opened his eyes and was surprised to find the maid standing before him, as graceful and bright as ever – yet altogether lifeless, as hard and cold as a block of stone.

Uncomprehending, he made his way down the hill, across the plain, through the forest and back to his village. Since he could not court or marry the maid of silver, he would have no other and he died of a broken heart, in the passing of the days.

But from that time on, you may look carefully into the night sky and see the Silver Maid's reflection and her milk spilled by the wind across the Milky Way.

THE GIRL AND THE MOON MAN

There once lived among the Chukchi a man who had only one child, a daughter who was as pale as a moonbeam.

Each summer she would keep her lonely vigil with her father's herd of deer, far from the camping grounds. And when winter came she would move her deer even farther away to pastures new. When hunger overtook her she would return to her father, riding a sturdy red deer.

On one such night, as she was riding back to the camping grounds, the red deer cried:

'Look, look, Mistress, the Moon Man comes!'

As the girl lifted her head, she saw the Moon Man descending to earth in a reindeer-drawn sledge.

'What is his mission?' she asked.

'To carry you off,' the deer replied.

The girl was afraid.

'What am I to do?'

Without a word, the red deer raked away the snow with his hoof until he had scooped out a large hole.

'Come, hide in this hole, quick!' he said.

The girl hopped into the hole, and the deer swiftly kicked snow over her head so that very soon she was completely covered. All that remained was a mound of snow.

The Moon Man came down from the sky, pulled up his reindeer and walked all around, glancing about him for the girl. He even went up to the mound of snow, sniffed at it, peered at it – yet he never guessed what it was.

'Wherever can she be?' he exclaimed. 'I cannot see her anywhere.'

With an irritable sigh, he climbed into his sledge and rode back up the dark curtain of night into the sky.

The moment he was gone, the red deer scraped the snow from the girl and she sprang out.

'Come, we must go to the camp quickly,' he said, 'for the Moon Man will surely be back in a while.'

The girl climbed upon the deer's back and off they rode in a swirl of snowflakes. In no time at all, they reached the camp and the girl hastened to her father's yaranga. Alas: no one was home.

Who would save her now?

Again the red deer came to her aid.

'I will turn you into a block of stone so that the Moon Man will not find you,' he said.

'No, no, that won't do,' she replied. 'He will know it is me.'

'A hammer then.'

'That won't do either,' she cried.

'A tent pole.'

'No.'

'A hair on the tent flap.'

'No, no.'

Then she had an idea.

'I know, turn me into a lamp.'

As she crouched in the form of a lamp, the deer struck the ground with his hoof and, instantly, the girl was turned into a lamp. It burned brightly, giving light to the whole tent.

Meanwhile the Moon Man, who had been seeking the girl among the herd of deer, came racing into the camp. He tethered his reindeer, entered the tent and set to searching it from top to bottom. He peered in between the tent poles, he examined every pot and pan, every hair on the hides, every twig under the beds, every knot of the bed planks, every grain of soil upon the floor. Yet the girl was nowhere to be seen.

As for the lamp, he did not notice it at all: for though it shone brightly, the Moon Man's glow was even brighter.

'Wherever can she be?' he kept muttering to himself.

Finally, he gave up and left the tent to return to his sledge.

Hardly had he climbed into it than he heard a peal of merry laughter from the tent.

'Here I am, here I am!' the girl called, poking her head out.

Straightaway the Moon Man rushed back into the tent. But the girl had once again turned back into the lamp. His fury mounting, the Moon Man looked among the kindling, and among the leaves, and among the strands of wool, and among the contents of the night vessel, and in every breath of air – but she was nowhere.

'Wherever can she be?' he cried.

Again he gave up. And no sooner had he left the tent than the girl grew bold and poked her head through the tent flap.

'Here I am, here I am,' she called, with a laugh.

In a frenzy, the Moon Man fairly rushed into the tent and began his search anew, this time even more thoroughly than before. He turned everything over two or three times, even peering into every sound and silence. But he could not find her.

So weary did he become from his searchings that he began to wane: his plump figure soon shrivelled away until he could barely move his spindly arms and legs.

Seeing him thus, the girl was no longer afraid. She took on her proper form, seized the Moon Man and threw him on to his back. Then she bound his hands and feet.

'Ooooh! Oooo!' groaned the shadow of the Moon Man. 'I wished to carry you off. Now I must die for my wickedness. Pray, cover me with sealskins that I may warm myself before I perish. I am so chilled.'

The girl was much surprised.

'You – chilled?' she exclaimed. 'Why, you dwell beneath the open sky; you have no yaranga, no home at all. What need have you of sealskins?'

Thereupon he began to weep and plead with the girl.

'I am homeless and doomed to roam the skies forever. Let me go, I beg you, and I shall help your people always. Let me free and I shall turn night into day. Let me free and I shall measure all the months of the year for you. And folk will say: that is the Moon of the Old Buck,

The Cold Udder Moon,
Genuine Udder Moon,
Calving Moon,
The Moon of the Waters,
The Making Leaves Moon,
The Moon of Warmth,
The Velvet Antlers Moon,
The Moon of Love among the Wild Deer,
The Moon of the First Winter,
Muscles of the Back Moon,
And the Shrinking Days Moon.'

'If I let you go, you will regain your strength,' said the girl. 'And when the marrow in your bones is fat and strong, once more you will come down for me.'

'No, no, never, I swear!' cried the Moon Man. 'I shall never forget the wisdom and spirit of Chukchi maids. You are too clever for me. I promise never to come down from the skies again.'

So the girl let him go and he rose high into the sky and at once lit up the heavens and the earth. From that time on he served the Chukchi as he had promised.

And he serves them still.

MERGEN AND HIS FRIENDS

Long ago by the swift-flowing River Amur lived Mergen, a bold Nanai hunter. Though he would never slay more than met his needs, his table never lacked for food.

One day his hunting led him far from home. Having encountered no prey for his deadly bow, he pushed deep into the taiga where the fierce old snow tiger roamed. As he pressed on through the forest, he suddenly came upon a deer stuck fast in a swamp. Pleased at good fortune at last, he was about to loose an arrow at the beast when it spoke to him in a human voice:

'Spare me, Mergen, please pull me out of this swamp.'

The hunter took pity on the deer and pulled it free of the clinging mud. Shaking itself clean, the deer said gratefully:

'Mergen, should you ever need me, just call my name and I shall come at once.'

So saying, it vanished into the trees. Mergen continued through the untamed taiga, his keen eyes seeking any movement amid the ferns and bushes. Presently, he came upon an ant trapped by the fallen branch. The little ant begged him:

'Save me, Mergen, please free me from this trap.'

Feeling sorry for the little ant, Mergen lifted the branch and set the ant free.

'Thank you, Mergen,' the ant said. 'You have only to call me when you are in need and I shall come to your aid.'

Mergen made his way along the banks of the Amur until he came to a shallow pool. There he sat down to wash the dust from his face, drink the cool water and rest. But no sooner had he unfastened his quiver than a hoarse voice wheezed:

'Save me, Mergen, I'm dying. I've been lying here these three days past.'

Looking down, Mergen saw a big sturgeon stranded in the shallows. Without a thought, he thrust his shoulder against the fish's side and pushed it hard towards the river's course. As its tail touched the rushing waters, the sturgeon swished it hard and dived deep into the Amur's raging torrents.

As Mergen settled back to rest, the sturgeon's great head rippled the river's surface.

'Thank you, Mergen,' it said. 'Should you ever need my help, just call my name.'

After he had rested, the hunter continued on his way until he emerged from the trees into a large clearing. And there before him stood a cluster of tents of an unfamiliar clan. An old man appeared from the grandest tent and advanced to greet him.

'Who are you?' the old man asked.

'I am a hunter from the Nanai tribe,' replied Mergen. 'I was hunting in the taiga and came unexpectedly upon your camp.'

'Then stay with us and rest,' said the old man, pulling on his pipe and smiling artfully.

Hardly had Mergen entered the old man's yaranga than he heard the tinkling of bronze earrings behind him. Glancing round he saw in the doorway the most beautiful maiden he had ever seen. She smiled a wistful, sighing smile that pierced the hunter's heart. There was something sad and mysterious about the lovely girl who stood there in the doorway, her long black braid hanging almost to her feet.

'Well,' said the old man, puffing on his pipe, 'what do you think of my daughter?'

'Many Nanai beauties dwell upon the banks of the Amur, but I have never set eyes on one so fair,' confessed the simple-hearted Mergen, 'I would readily take her for my wife.'

'You should know that a hundred or more bold hunters before you have sought her hand,' said the old man. 'And they are all now my servants. But you may try your luck, if you wish. I shall set you three tasks: should you pass these tests, you will be my son. Should you fail, you will become my slave like all the others.'

'Agreed,' said Mergen without a thought.

'My loyal servants, bring me my iron boots!' shouted the old man.

And straightaway servants came running to bring in the heavy boots.

'Take these boots,' the old man said, 'and should you wear them out in a single night, you may come to me for your second task.'

Taking the boots, Mergen went alone into the taiga.

'I'd surely have to walk a hundred miles in a hundred lives to wear out boots like these,' he reflected sadly. Then, suddenly, he recalled his friend the deer.

'Deer, my friend, come to my aid!' he cried.

And before the echo had died away, the deer was standing before him. Mergen recounted his adventures and, without a word, the deer pulled the boots on its hind legs and dashed off into the hills, leaving a trail of stars and comets across the dark sky. In the meantime, Mergen lay upon the moss and fell asleep. When he awoke at dawn, the deer was already grazing by his side.

All that remained of the iron boots were tattered tops.

Mergen was overjoyed. Kissing his fleet-footed friend upon its velvet nose, he seized the tattered boot-tops and hastened to the camp. When he reached the master's tent, he shouted noisily from without until the old man appeared.

Hurling the boot-tops at his feet, Mergen exclaimed:

'There, tell me my second task!'

For a moment, the old man was silent. Then he shouted:

'Servants, fetch me five sacks of millet!'

When the grain was brought, he shook it out upon the soil so that the grains scattered far and wide across the camp. Then he chuckled gleefully:

'Now gather up all the millet so that not a single grain is lost. You have just one day to complete the task.'

Mergen returned to the forest, sat down upon a mossy mound and called:

'Little ant, my friend, come to my aid.'

In no time at all, the little ant appeared and listened to the hunter's request. Thereupon, summoning the entire tribe of ants, he soon had the whole earth teeming with ants – so many that they covered every grain of soil in the camp. Before Mergen had smoked a pipeful of tobacco, every grain of millet had been returned to the sacks from whence it had come.

Thanking the ants, Mergen strode boldly back to the old man. The master was even more amazed; scratching his head, he said:

'I shall set you one final task. If you succeed, my daughter will be yours. Now listen to what I have to say: many moons past, when I was a boy, my father dropped a golden ring into the river. You have until dusk to find it.'

Mergen left the tent crestfallen, but was cheered by the sight of the maid waving to him from behind the tent. And he strode boldly towards the riverbank.

'Sturgeon, my friend,' he called into the deep, 'come to my aid.'

Thrice he called down into the depths of the waters before the Amur bubbled and boiled, and the sturgeon's great head thrust through the waters.

Mergen told it of his task.

Without a word, the sturgeon dived to the riverbed and summoned every creature that swam in the river. Fish big and small darted to and fro along the bottom of the river until the ring was found.

The delighted hunter bore the golden ring back to the old man. Astonished, the old master took the ring and disappeared back into his yaranga. Presently he re-emerged, his radiant daughter by his side.

'Here you are, bold Mergen, I am true to my word. Take my only daughter as your wife; and take my servants, my camp and myself. We are yours.'

Said Mergen in reply:

'I thank you, Father. But from this day forth there shall be no servants. Let us all be brothers and live in peace.'

And so it was. Thenceforth the Nanai tribes have lived in peace and brotherhood along the banks of the River Amur.

COOT AND THE FOX

When Coot was a tailor he spent his time sewing. One day he was sitting at the tent door making himself a pair of trousers when something came between him and the light.

'What can it be?' thought God. 'I know, it must be my nose. How annoying.'

So he took a knife and cut off his nose. Then he returned to his sewing but still something blocked the light.

'I know, it must be my cheeks,' Coot told himself. 'I'll have to cut them off too.'

So he took his knife and cut off his cheeks. But this did not help either; his face was beginning to give him pain and he was soon moaning and sighing and doing little else. Happening to glance out of the tent, he spied some baby mice playing by the tent opening.

'So that's who blocked the light,' Coot cried.

'I see you are having fun rolling about, little ones,' he said. 'Now why don't you let me give you a ride in these trousers?'

And he held out the trousers he had been sewing. But the mice were suspicious.

'You might catch us and eat us if we did,' they said.

'I won't do you any harm,' Coot assured them. 'I only want to give you a ride.'

The mice were reassured by these words and did as Coot suggested; thereupon the tailor quickly sewed up the trousers so that they could not climb out, and he carried them off to the forest. Looking for a tall tree, he found one at last and said:

> *'Come, tree,*
> *Bend down to me.'*

102

The tree bent down and Coot hung the trousers from its topmost branch. Then he ordered:

> *'Now, tree,*
> *Stand properly.'*

At once the tree stood back upright and Coot went home, leaving the mice squeaking loudly in fear.

By and by a fox came running up, attracted by all the squealing.

'Why do you make such a noise, mice?' she asked.

'Because of what Coot did to us,' the mice replied, and they told the fox how they had been playing by Coot's tent, how he had got them to climb into the trousers, how he had sewn them up and hung them on the tree.

'What did Coot say before hanging you there?' the fox asked.

> *'Come, tree,*
> *Bend down to me.'*

'That's all he said,' called the mice.

So the fox repeated:

> *'Come, tree,*
> *Bend down to me.'*

Instantly the tree bent down, and the fox made a hole in the trousers and let out the mice. All were alive and well except for one tiny mouse who had been trampled on by the others and had fainted.

The fox instructed the mice to gather pieces of rotting wood and to put them with the sick mouse on top inside the trousers. This they did.

'Now, mice, tell me,' said the fox again. 'What did Coot say after hanging you on the tree?'

> *'Now, tree,*
> *Stand properly.'*

'That's all he said,' chattered the mice together.

So the fox cried:

> *'Now, tree,*
> *Stand properly.'*

Straightaway the tree stood upright and the fox led the mice off to her house. When they arrived, the fox gave orders for them to bring any scraps of food they could find, along with pine cones and pieces of bark, and to put them all in the trough that was standing in the corner. The mice did so, and then all ran away to hide in the loft.

Two days passed and on the third Coot rose very early and set out for the tall tree in the forest. He skipped gaily along feeling as pleased as could be that he would have some tender mice to eat for dinner.

He came to the tree where he had left the mice and told it to bend down; and when it did, he made a small hole in the trousers, put his hand through and pulled out the sick mouse. Now, that mouse had long since come out of its faint, but, finding itself in Coot's hands, it lay very still pretending to be dead.

'Good, the mice are still there,' Coot cried, feeling the weight of the trousers. 'My wife Mitti and I will have a fine mouse dinner.'

He put the mouse back in the trousers and sewed up the hole he had made, not noticing that the little mouse had slipped out and scuttled away.

'How heavy these dead mice are,' he said to himself as he walked along. 'They were much lighter when they were alive.'

When he got home he told Mitti to make up the fire, saying to her:

'We'll lie down and rest for a while and then have our supper later.'

They lay down on the bed and the fox, who had been following Coot, watched from behind the door. As soon as Coot and Mitti were snoring loudly, the fox gathered up some thorns and spread them over the floor. Then she ran home, smeared her face with alder dye and waited.

Presently, Coot woke up and nudged Mitti.

'Time to get up, Mitti,' he said. 'Let's boil some of those plump mice, so that we can eat to our heart's content.'

Mitti sprang out of bed but, alas for her, stepped straight on a thorn.

'Oh, oh, oh!' she cried.

'What's the matter, you silly woman?' called Coot irritably.

Poor Mitti only groaned. Picking up Coot's trousers, she ripped them open and let out another groan.

'Someone's fooled you, Coot,' she cried. 'There were no mice here, just pieces of rotten wood.'

'That's impossible!' Coot shouted. 'Why, I took a dead mouse out of the trousers myself in the forest.'

He sprang out of bed and he too stepped on a thorn, and he hopped about the floor among the scattered thorns, shouting with pain. He snatched up his trousers and saw that Mitti had indeed been speaking the truth, for they were filled with pieces of rotten wood. Coot was very angry and realized that it must have been his old enemy the fox who had tricked him.

'Give me the poker, Mitti,' he exclaimed. 'I'm going to deal with that vixen once and for all.'

Mitti handed him the poker and Coot set out for the fox's house. He reached it soon enough and as he approached he heard loud groans coming from within.

'Are you ill that you are moaning so, fox?' he asked. 'I have come to see you about those mice that were taken from the tree. You know something of that, I'll be bound.'

'Oh no, Coot, I know nothing of it,' simpered the fox, in a weak voice. 'I've been very, very sick and unable to go out for a whole month past. Do you see that trough over there? It's full of rubbish, but I haven't the strength even to empty it. I wish some kind person would do it for me.'

The simple Coot felt sorry for the fox.

'Then I'll do it,' he offered.

'Thank you, neighbor,' murmured the fox. 'I'll never forget your kindness. As soon as I am well I'll help you all I can. But there is one thing: do not look back as you are carrying the trough out, for you might drop it if you do, and then think of all the trouble you'll have picking up the mess.'

Coot picked up the trough and took it out, but as he did not look behind him, he could not see that the fox was following him.

They came to a hill and climbed to the top, and as Coot lifted the trough to throw down the rubbish, the fox gave him such a shove that he toppled down the hillside . . . trough, rubbish and all.

The fox came home and let the mice down from the loft, and they lived in peace to the end of their days, for Coot was much too scared ever to go near them again.

FATHER OF SICKNESS

One of our kinsmen, Nya Nganas, went walking one day in the snow-clad taiga to look for game. But the spirits were not with him and he caught nothing. All of a sudden, however, the day turned foggy and he could not find his way home.

Although he searched this way and that he could not find the homeward path and eventually came upon a stream which seemed to have come from nowhere. When he tried to jump across he lost his footing and plunged into the water. Down and down he sank, far into the depths, until at last he came out on the other side, underneath the water.

The land there stretched to the horizon without a trace of snow; just the tips of the grass were slightly whitened as if touched by hoare frost.

He set out to cross this strange new land, looking to all sides for some sign of life. At last he spotted a young girl traveling along a track in front of him. She was riding a strangely colored reindeer. As he ran after her, he called out:

'Hello there, from what tribe are you?'

But the girl did not seem to hear him, for she paid no heed. As he caught up with her he touched her lightly on the shoulder.

'Who are you?' he asked.

At his touch the girl cried out in pain.

'Why does my shoulder hurt so, as if someone is stabbing me?' she cried.

'What a strange girl?' Nya Nganas said, 'She certainly looks like a girl from our parts, yet whatever I say she doesn't hear me.'

So again he tapped her on the shoulder and once more she let out a cry of pain:

'Oh, oh! An evil spirit sickness has pierced my shoulder.'

107

'What a strange thing,' thought Nya Nganas. 'I'll travel behind her and see where she's bound.'

On and on they went, with the girl constantly crying and groaning. Finally, a camp of some five or six chooms came into view: they were of the Tungus people. Arriving at the tents, the girl entered one of them, crying loudly:

'A sickness spirit struck me along the way.'

Nya Nganas followed the girl into the choom and sat down behind the tent pole some way from her.

'Where did the spirit strike you?' the girl was asked.

But she cried out in great pain and was too poorly to explain. So sorry for her did our man feel that he tried to wrap her in his parka despite her shrieks of pain.

All the while the fire in the hearth crackled and hissed as if hostile to the visitor.

The people in the choom said:

'Why is the fire behaving so? Why does it crackle and hiss? Something evil has entered our choom: the spirit sickness has come. What shall we do? Our poor maid will not last long unless we do something.'

One of the girl's brothers then spoke up:

'Let us send for the old shaman who lives in the next camp; he may be able to cure our sister.'

It being agreed, he went off to fetch the shaman, returning with him that evening. The shaman was a wizened old man who at once began to weave his shaman spells and to talk with the spirits. Finally, he said:

'Three days will pass and the girl will get better.'

Thereupon, the shaman returned to his own choom. But the girl continued to moan as one gravely ill: day and night she lay in a fever and at the end of three days was even worse than before.

All the time, our man sat uncomprehending in the corner unseen by all.

At last, the girl's father spoke up:

'Our daughter is doomed, the old shaman could do nothing for her. Somewhere I've heard there is a young orphan who has become a shaman; he even has his drum and powerful charms. Let us summon him.'

The old man's eldest son again went forth and this time brought back the young shaman. Sitting alongside the girl, the orphan-shaman first took a bite to eat, then laid out his shaman's attire and drum upon the floor ready for his work. Having eaten, he began to pull on the shaman's bakari, the long fur boots. As he tied the laces of his boots, he stole a glance towards Nya Nganas. Having put on the remainder of his attire, he began to do up the thongs of his robe and again stole a glance in the direction of our man.

And our man thought to himself:

'This shaman knows I'm here.'

The shaman finished his dressing and now took up the drum; yet he still refrained from playing it. Nya Nganas meanwhile tried to hide behind the girl, pressing his face close to the girl's back so that the shaman should not see it. First from one side, then from the other, however, the shaman peered behind the girl as he beat his drum.

Beating the drum now very hard and fast, he chanted loudly:

'A sickness spirit has come. It came to you on the road and pierced your left shoulder. Do I speak truly?'

'You do,' whispered the girl.

'You have the sickness of *koga nguo*, the evil one,' continued the shaman; and turning to our man, he said, 'How is it, Nya Nganas, that you cling so tightly to the girl? You will tear out her soul. Tell us what it is you want; you shall have it, but let the girl go free.'

'Give me the strangely colored reindeer on which the girl rode here,' our man said. 'Give me that and I shall depart at once.'

The shaman now addressed the girl's father:

'The sickness spirit asks for the reindeer the girl rode. Do you give your consent?'

'Yes, certainly, certainly,' said the old man quickly.

'Good, it is settled,' said the young shaman. 'Now, brothers and sisters of the Tungus tribe, you must make a reindeer out of wood.'

So they set to making a reindeer out of wood; legs and horns and tail. And with the charred wood from the fire they drew patterns on its body. When the job was done, the shaman took up his drum and beat it loudly jumping up and down as if running fast. Our man, Nya Nganas, quite lost his senses from the drumming and dancing; he thought to himself:

'They've prepared the reindeer for me, I must mount it and get away from here.'

And he climbed on the wooden reindeer's back and galloped away like the wind across the plain.

All the while the shaman played his drum and danced round and round in circles until he dropped down exhausted. At the same time, far, far away on the bank of a stream, our man came to a sudden halt on his reindeer. When he looked about him, he found to his surprise that he was sitting on a wooden reindeer on the bank of the self-same stream upon which he had stumbled in the fog.

'What sort of shaman did this to me?' he wondered. 'The old shaman was not powerful at all; he did not even see me. But that young orphan-shaman was very strong; he made me lose my senses.'

Slipping down from the reindeer, he left it on the riverbank and walked home, soon coming to his choom. Once there he told his kinsfolk of his adventures in that other world.

'So I learned that some of us really are sickness spirits,' he said in conclusion. 'One of you, my brothers, is a piercing sickness; another is a fever sickness, and another the terrible smallpox spirit. One of us, it may be, will one day find himself in that other world, and then the same orphan-shaman will not let him go. He is a very clever shaman.'

With these words, everyone present turned into sickness spirits. No longer were they our people, they had each and every one become a sickness.

Henceforth, when someone is ill, folk say it is one of our kind who has come. And if the shaman cannot help, it is because he is like the weak old shaman. But should our sickness spirit find itself in a choom visited by the young orphan-shaman then he will see it and the spirit won't be able to steal a single soul.

WHO IS STRONGEST?

There was once a lad who was mighty curious about all he saw. Whysandwhatfors people called him; he was forever pestering them with his questions:

Why do deer grow trees on their heads?

Why does smoke fall into the sky and melt?

What makes snowflakes fly?

And so on and so on.

One time, the Whysandwhatfors boy went to his father and asked:

'Father, who is strongest?'

'Go to the stream and ask, my son,' replied his father.

So the boy left his father's tent, descended to the stream and found it covered in ice. Stepping across it, he suddenly slipped and fell on his back. Sore and bruised, he cried:

'Ice, why did you knock me over? You must be very strong.'

The ice rasped back in a loud voice:

'So I am if I can toss you about like dandelion fluff!'

But the boy had not gained his nickname for nothing: for he persisted:

'You are certainly strong, but why are you afraid of the sun? When spring comes, he melts you to water.'

Ice's face froze hard and he confessed that the sun was stronger.

The boy looked up at the sun and asked:

'Are you the strongest?'

'I must be strong,' said the sun, with a wink, 'if I can vanquish the ice.'

Yet the boy was not satisfied.

'If you are strongest, why can even a tiny cloud blot you out?'

111

The sun scowled.

'Because clouds are stronger than I am,' he had to admit.

Next the boy addressed a cloud:

'Cloud, are you strongest?'

'So it would seem if even the sun fears me,' it replied.

'Then why do you flee through the sky before the wind?' asked the inquisitive boy.

A frown darkened the cloud as he called back:

'That's because the wind must be stronger than me.'

So the boy talked to the wind:

'Wind, are you the strongest?'

'If you please,' said the wind, 'since I can scatter the clouds to the four winds.'

'But if you are so strong, why can you not move mountains?' the lad persisted.

'Because,' the wind rumbled, 'they are stronger than me.'

On ran the boy to the mountains.

'Hello, tall mountains,' he called. 'If the wind cannot shift you, you must be very strong.'

'So we are,' they roared. All the same, they had to admit that they could not stop trees growing on their slopes. The trees therefore were stronger.

Turning to the trees, the boy asked his question.

'Yes, we are certainly strong if the mountains cannot uproot us,' they replied.

'Then why do you fall when man chops you down?' the boy asked.

A great murmur spread through the trees as they sighed:

'Do you not know the answer by now? Man is stronger than us. He is the strongest in the world.'

At last the boy was satisfied. Now he knew that there was none stronger than man. Quickly he ran home to tell his father the lesson he had learned.

CHOLEREE

There once lived a brother and sister with their little dog. So fond of its master was the dog that it followed him everywhere: when he went hunting, the dog went too.

One time the brother left his sister at home and went off to hunt with his faithful friend. As they came to a lake, the boy caught a wild duck and was about to kill it when the duck spoke to him in a human voice:

'Do not kill me; one day I may be able to help you.'

Being sorry for the duck, the hunter let it go and returned home, his pouch empty. Yet as he walked along, the dog began to whine and said in a voice full of pain:

'Master, there is something crawling on my leg. Should I die, you must cut me into six equal parts.'

The master was surprised.

'Why should I cut up my best friend?' he mused, searching in the dog's thick fur.

At last he found a big flea and squashed it. Straightaway the dog died.

The boy was sad to lose his friend, but he decided to carry out his last orders and cut the dog into six equal parts. That done, he left the pieces where the dog had died and returned home.

Next day, he came back to that same place and was surprised to find two wolves, two bears and two foxes devouring the dog meat. Even as he drew near the animals showed no sign of alarm; they came towards him, licked his hand and treated him as their master. So he led them all to his home.

From that day on, the six animals went everywhere with their master, just as the faithful dog had done before.

While he was away hunting one day, his sister went to the river for water and, as she filled her pails, she looked up and saw the evil, one-eyed, one-legged and one-armed monster Choleree sitting on the bank.

'Girl, I like the look of you,' said Choleree. 'I'd like to come and live with you.'

'Then come and welcome,' she said.

So the girl and Choleree set out together.

'When your brother comes home,' Choleree told her, 'make out you are sick. He will ask what ails you and you will say that you have a fever. Then he will feed you on fresh meat; but do not eat it. Tell him to go to his barns and bring you some dried fish. As soon as he leaves the house, you let me in.'

The girl promised to do as he said.

While Choleree hid in the forest, the girl returned home and lay on her bed, groaning loudly. As her brother arrived from hunting, she asked him to go to his barns for dried fish. So he went to the barns at once. Coming to one, he found the doors firmly closed with his two bears locked inside. Coming to the second, he found that the doors had taken root in the ground so that he could not pull them open; and his two wolves sat inside unable to get out. He went to the third and discovered that his two foxes were locked inside.

When he returned to the house, how shocked he was at the sight that greeted him: for there, sitting by his sister, was none other than the evil, one-eyed, one-legged, one-armed Choleree, gnashing his iron teeth and winking his lone eye in the center of his forehead.

'How glad I am you've come,' said Choleree. 'I've been looking forward to tasting your liver and innards. But I only eat fresh meat: go and scrub yourself clean in the bath-house before I eat you.'

What was the young man to do?

His animal friends could not help him; but then he recalled the wild duck whose life he had spared. Could it really save him from his plight? No sooner did the thought enter his head than the duck was already flying to him. In its flight, the duck thrust open all the barn doors with its wings, so freeing the bears, wolves and foxes who straightaway rushed to their master.

At once, the boy told his faithful friends of his predicament.

'Then do as Choleree says,' said the bears. 'But when you have washed, stay where you are and call Choleree to us in the bath-house.'

At that moment, his sister's voice was heard from inside the house.

'Brother, why are you so long? Choleree is starving.'

'Then tell him to come out here himself to the bath-house,' the boy replied.

Within the second, out of the house stepped the monster, sharpening his iron teeth as he came. No sooner had he crossed the threshold of the bath-house, though, than the two bears and the two wolves rushed at him and tore at him with their sharp teeth. Then the two foxes set upon him. Before long there was nothing left of the evil ogre but scraps of skin and gristle.

The young man lit the bath-house fire and burned what remained of Choleree. That done, he returned to the house and, taking his wicked sister by the arm, dragged her into the forest where he tied her to a tall tree. Before her he placed two pots.

'Should you weep for me, ashamed of your sins, then the right pot will fill with your tears and the left will turn upside down. Should you weep for Choleree, then the left pot will fill with your tears.'

So said the brother to his sister before departing.

Next morning, he came to see what had become of his sister. And there before him stood the left pot filled to the brim with tears, while the right one stood upside down.

He became very angry. Leaving his sister tied to the tree, he walked and walked wherever his anger took him. Eventually he arrived at a settlement, met a young girl and was soon wed. There he stayed and forgot all about his wicked sister.

Yet meanwhile, far away in the depths of the forest, his sister remained tied to the tall tree until the branches withered and died; then she dropped from the tree and made her way back to her old home. All she found was ashes: no house, no bath-house, no barns. Yet as she stood on the site of the old bath-house, she stubbed her toe against something hard and sharp: it was Choleree's iron teeth. Thrusting them into her bag, she set off to seek her brother.

After a time she arrived at the settlement where her brother was living, entered his new house and pretended to be a most loving and remorseful sister. As her brother got ready for bed that night, she told him:

'Brother, let me make the bed softer for you.'

She patted down the bed and put Choleree's sharp teeth under the covers.

The household lay down to sleep and all was still.

In the morning when the wife awoke she found her husband lying dead, his heart bitten right through.

The wife and sister mourned for a bit, then set to debating what to do with the body. The sister was all for burning her brother's remains, but the wife would have none of it.

'No,' she said, firmly. 'We shall put him in a hollow trunk and leave him in the trees, as our fathers did. We shall lay him in an iron-bound coffin and put it high out of reach of wild animals. And then we must bury your brother's animal companions in the ground alongside the tree.'

And so it was as the wife said. They put the dead man in an iron-bound coffin, placed the coffin in a tall tree and buried the animals by the tree.

'Oh, how dark it is!' said the animals, underground. 'How are we to escape from here?'

'Let the foxes dig a hole,' said the bears. 'After all, they dig their den in the ground.'

And the foxes began to dig a hole through the earth until they caught a glimpse of the daylight.

Then the wolves spoke up:

'Bears, you are skilled at digging holes too; help the foxes widen the hole for us all to squeeze through.'

So the bears set to work with the foxes and soon had made an opening wide enough for them all to squeeze through As they emerged into the sunlight, they saw the hollow trunk and iron-

116

bound coffin with their dead master high up in the tree.

'How shall we get that down?' they wondered.

'Perhaps the duck will help us?' suggested the bears.

No sooner were the words spoken than the duck appeared. It broke open the coffin with its strong wings and brought the master down to earth gently on its back. As the animals crowded round the still form of their old master, they noticed a wound in his chest from which the blood was still flowing.

'Let's try to heal the wound,' said the bears. 'You wolves run off swiftly and bring the water of life; you are the best runners among us.'

Off went the wolves for the water of life, while the other animals set to licking their master's wound. In no time at all the wolves were back with the life-giving water: as soon as they had bathed the wound in it, their master stood up as if nothing had happened.

Without more ado, he returned home and killed his wicked sister on the spot. Then he took up his old life together with his wife and his six devoted animal friends. And they all lived in peace and tolerance.

THE LITTLE WHALE

There once lived a hunter with two wives: the elder had children, the younger had none. As the husband spent all his time with the mother of his children, the younger wife grew lonely and came to spend much of her time walking along the seashore.

Early one morning, as she sat upon the shore lamenting her solitude and gazing wistfully out to sea at the sunrise, she spied a little fountain of water coming closer and closer to the shore.

It came from a large Greenland whale.

As the whale reached the beach, a man stepped from inside it and came towards her; she welcomed him gladly, talked and sat till dark with him.

From that time on she would spend her days in the yaranga pretending to be sick, then venture down to the shore each night the moment all others were asleep. It was not long before her husband found her out and one night followed her.

He watched as the young man emerged from the whale, was welcomed and given food by the young wife. Yet there was something wary in his manner; all of a sudden, he left his meal and rushed down to the sea where he had left his whale-skin. Just as he was pulling on his skin, the angry husband flung a harpoon straight at the whale, so piercing its side as it swam off. The wounded whale spurted a blood-red fountain into the air before disappearing into the waves.

And the whale-man was never seen again.

The young wife meanwhile was with child and soon after gave birth to a little whale. At first, they kept him in a leather bucket filled with water; but it was not long before they had to provide a bigger tank full of sea-water. Once that became too small they dug a deep hole outside the yaranga, smeared fat over the cracks and dropped stones in to cover the bottom; then they filled it with water and let the little whale live there until he had grown quite big. And when he was too large for that they dragged him down to the water's edge and left him there.

Before letting him go, however, they sewed a squirrel-skin flap over his blow-hole so that he could be recognized when he blew his fountain.

At first he swam close by the shore afraid to venture too far out to sea; he would swim on to the beach where his mother fed him from her breast. But with the passage of time he became bolder and began to feed himself from the sea.

One day in autumn he swam away with another whale, yet returned the following spring with a large school of whales, bringing them right into shore where the Nunegnint tribe could kill them. Soon the Nunegnints began to boast of all the whales they had caught thanks to the little whale who guided so many to their harpoons. They slew so many whales that they never lacked for meat or light throughout the barren winter. But their neighbors, the Memrepints, became very envious.

One day, a band of Memrepints crept up on the little whale and killed him. It was not long before the Nunegnints missed their little whale and discovered what had happened. They were determined to take their revenge. Shortly after, when the strongest of the Memrepint hunters was fishing alone on his kayak close by the cliffs, a group of Nunegnints set upon him, shooting him dead with their bows.

From then on the two tribes lived at war.

Even today, a cheat or a bully is teased with the name of the neighboring tribe, the Memrepint or the Nunegnint. And the deep hole by the yaranga where the baby whale was kept can still be seen.

BOLD YATTO AND HIS SISTER TAYUNE

Far into the cold night on the shores of the great Arctic Sea is a land of dark shadows. And above that forbidding land the Sun is drawn across the sky in a sleigh pulled by a reindeer with golden antlers. Though this does not happen often. For the evil witch Blizzard lays her icy hand upon the earth, blotting out the daylight and raging through the long Arctic night.

Long, long ago, on the shores of the Arctic Sea stood an old deerskin yaranga, where a poor woman lived with her son Yatto and her daughter Tayune. She had no husband to protect and fend for them, since he had drowned in the spring. So the mother did all the work herself.

One day she fell ill and asked her son to fetch the firewood. Without fire they would all perish. But Yatto snuggled under his deerskin cover and pretended he had not heard his mother's plea.

'Daughter, fetch some firewood,' said Mother. 'Should the fire go out, the evil witch Blizzard will come and freeze us all!'

'I'm too busy,' replied Tayune, fussing with her long black braids.

Blizzard was now quite close.

Yet there was still life in the fading embers of the fire. A spark flying in the night breeze fell on Blizzard's snowy robe, and burned a jagged hole in it.

Blizzard was afraid of fire.

With a sighing hiss, the fire went out at last. At once Blizzard swept into the yaranga and banged her icy stick upon the floor. Poor Mother rose from her plank bed and lifted her weak arms to

120

shield her children . . . But at that moment her arms turned to wings.

As Blizzard waved her stick before the children, their mother, now a broad-winged seagull, protected them with her black-tipped wings. But, in a swirl of cold mist, Blizzard enveloped the seagull and swept her away. And Yatto and Tayune were left alone.

'It's all your fault,' cried Tayune.

'No, it's yours,' said Yatto.

There was no point in quarreling. Mother was gone and they had to sit the whole night through shivering by the cold hearth. And in the morning, Yatto took his bow and arrows, tied on his snow shoes and said to his sister:

'Come, we must find Mother and rescue her.'

In the meantime, Blizzard had taken the seagull to her ice yaranga; she banged her stick upon the ground and the bird took human form once more.

'Now you will make me a new robe to replace this scorched one,' ordered Blizzard.

Mother set to work. Her hands were soon stiff with cold from the ice cloth and the ice needle. Yet all the while her thoughts were of her children: how would they fare without her? Who would make up the fire in the tent?

By now, Yatto and Tayune were far from home. The kind old Sun had shown them the way.

'Blizzard dwells in the icy mountains,' he told the children. 'The way there is long and arduous. Here, take these three arrows; they will help you should misfortune befall you.'

Three shining arrows fell at Yatto's feet. The boy picked them up, wrapped them carefully in a deerskin and put them inside his fur jacket, as polar night descended upon the tundra.

Just then, a baby deer emerged from the gloom, his eyes wide with fear because a wolf was close upon his heels. At once Yatto seized one of the Sun's arrows and fired it at the wolf, scaring him away. And the baby fell in with the children for he too had lost his mother.

But Blizzard, who sees all and knows all, sent Giant Sleepyhead to lull the children with his magic horn. Unfortunately for Blizzard that giant was always falling asleep himself. And so it was: as he lay down to rest Tayune stole up and took away his magic horn, and she played a tune that soon had the giant snoring in the snow.

The three journeyed on until they saw Mother Deer come bounding towards them. So pleased was she at finding her little son that she set the two children upon her back and ran off faster than the wind until they reached the icy mountains. There the children bade farewell to the deer, and climbed to the very top of the mountain where Blizzard's yaranga stood. Through its crystal walls the children could see their mother, sitting and sewing and shivering. But between the yaranga and the children yawned a great abyss.

How were they to cross it?

Tayune had an idea. She cut off her lovely long braids, her pride and joy, and wove them quickly into a rope. Then, Yatto made a loop in one end like a lasso, and threw it right across the abyss so that it landed over an icy outcrop.

At that very moment, Blizzard sent Darkness to envelop the children in her velvet folds and blot out every glimmer of light. Quick as a flash, brave Yatto shot the Sun's second arrow into the sky and, in an instant, the Sun's three giant brothers, the Northern Lights, appeared, each holding aloft a glittering torch.

Darkness retreated.

Yatto and his sister Tayune made their way across the braided rope. But on the other side, outside her yaranga, stood the terrible figure of Blizzard herself.

'Come not a step farther or you will die! she cried.

Yatto shot his last arrow at her. It pierced her icy heart and she melted clean away.

Mother at once came running from the yaranga to greet her children.

'You have become a real hunter, my son,' she said. 'I'm so proud of you.'

Turning to Tayune, she asked, 'Where are those long braids you treasured so much, my daughter?'

'Never mind, Mother,' Tayune replied, with a smile, 'they will grow again. You are safe, that is all that matters.'

So the three returned to their home on the shore of the great Arctic Sea, happy and more than a whit wiser.

AIPANANA AND ETUVGI

In a time gone by, there lived two trappers in neighboring camps: Aipanana and Etuvgi. One day, at just the same hour, they left their yarangas to go hunting in the tundra.

Aipanana tracked a wild reindeer and finally brought it down with his third arrow. Meanwhile, Etuvgis set a wolf trap and caught a big grey wolf.

Aipanana set to skinning his reindeer and praising the beast: 'What a magnificent hide – the best there is for sure.'

At the same time, Etuvgi was skinning his wolf and praising his good fortune:

'What a wonderful warm pelt – there's surely none better.'

Aipanana thrust the deer meat into his sack, tossed the skin over his shoulder and stepped out cheerily for home.

And Etuvgi hoisted the wolfskin on to his shoulder and made for home with a springy step.

Since their homeward trails crossed, it was not long before the two hunters met and hailed one another.

'Good day to you, friend,' said Etuvgi. 'You've a grand deer hide there, I see.'

'And it's a splendid wolfskin you've got yourself, answered the other.

One sang the praises of the deer, the other lauded the wolf. And so it continued.

'Your wolf has such a big warm pelt,' said Aipanana.

'But your deerskin is such a handsome color,' rejoined Etuvgi. 'Only . . . the wolfskin is thicker than the deerskin, don't you think?'

Aipanana frowned.

'No,' he said firmly. 'The deerskin is thicker than the wolfskin.'

'Nonsense,' exclaimed Etuvgi. 'See here, my wolfskin is much thicker.'

'Now, hold on,' said Aipanana, getting rather tetchy, 'this deerskin is thicker, I tell you.'

And so the argument went on, loud and long, with each hunter becoming more stubborn than the other.

Finally, Etuvgi said in exasperation:

'All right, there's only one way to settle this: we'll see which skin has more hairs – the wolf or the deer.'

Aipanana nodded.

So they sat down in the snow, set the hides before them and began to count.

Etuvgi plucked hair after hair from his wolfskin and set each to one side.

Aipanana plucked hair after hair from his deerskin and laid them in a row.

Their counting began in the light of morning and continued all through the day into the dark of night. A new morning dawned as the two men continued their counting. And they did not notice. The next day went by, and then another and another. Hunters passed by in the tracks of deer and polar fox; men hunted whale and seal and walrus; fishermen caught fish; their wives sewed new clothes, made pots and bows.

All the while Aipanana and Etuvgi went on counting and counting. And every now and then, they would glance at one another and say:

'My hide has more hairs than yours, I tell you.'

And the one would not give way, and the other would not give way.

Both grew haggard from hunger, both grew feeble from fatigue. Some folk say they still sit there to this day, plucking hairs from the wolf and the deer, placing them in rows and counting.

THE EIGHT BROTHERS

So this is the way it was.

Long ago there lived eight brothers who hunted whale. Fortune often smiled on them and they rarely lacked bone to frame their yaranga, oil to light their lamps and fat to feed the clan.

One day the brothers went out in their canoe after a big whale and were already in the open sea before they managed to spear the beast. But it was too heavy to haul back to shore. As they struggled with the carcass, a strong breeze was all the while blowing their little craft farther and farther out to sea. In desperation they finally decided to cut loose the dead whale.

But it was too late.

Night found them far out to sea. It was so dark that they could see nothing about them and they realized they were doomed. Yet, all of a sudden, the prow of the canoe bumped against a hard object and they were relieved to find themselves on a sandy shore.

The eldest brother called to the brother at the prow:

'Jump out and look around. See where we are. And see if you can find some fresh water, I'm so thirsty.'

Shortly after the brother had disappeared into the gloom, he shouted out:

'Oh, how good, oh how sweet and cool!'

And then he was silent.

'What's so good and sweet out there?' asked the eldest brother in surprise. 'Go and see,' he said to the next brother.

The second brother went ashore and no sooner had he vanished into the gloom than he, too, was heard to shout:

'Oh, how good, oh how sweet and cool!'

And he also fell silent like the first.

'What the devil's so good and sweet?' cried the eldest, quickly dispatching another brother. 'Only do be careful!' he cautioned.

Off went the third brother and presently exclaimed:

'Oh, how good, oh how sweet and cool!'

And he too failed to return.

'What is it they've found?' wondered the eldest brother. 'Go and take a look,' he ordered the fourth brother.

But in no time at all the remaining brothers again heard,

'Oh, how good, oh how sweet and cool!'

When the fourth brother did not appear, the eldest sent the fifth.

'Only take care,' he warned. 'Come back the moment you find something.'

Off went the fifth brother and immediately shouted:

'Oh, how good, oh how sweet and cool!'

But he too was lost.

'What is going on?' wondered the eldest, and sent the sixth brother.

Yet, like the others, he too vanished into thin air.

Now only two remained: the youngest and the eldest.

'Little brother,' said the eldest, 'wait here for me while I go to see what all this is about. Go nowhere; I'll be right back.'

And he was soon engulfed in the dark folds of night.

Suddenly a cry rang out:

'Oh, how good, oh how sweet and cool!'

And all was still.

'What am I to do now, all by myself,' wondered the youngest brother. 'But I won't move from here even if I have to die in the boat.'

He lay down in the bottom of the boat and suddenly heard a voice from above him:

'Hey, lad, look up here.'

Up jumped the boy, glanced all about him and shook his head in puzzlement; and then at last he saw in the sky the brightest star shining straight down on him. And he heard the voice again, this time from the star.

'Step ashore and crawl on your hands and knees. Do not follow your brothers' footsteps, take the path to the right. You and your brothers have come to the Land of Gloom, the Land of the Dead. And when they went ashore, your seven brothers were seized by the kelets who crept up on them from the left and stole their souls away. Go straight ahead and when you stumble over a mound, press it with your finger and drink your fill.'

The star fell silent.

So the young lad got out of the boat, crept along on his hands and knees, and when he faltered over a mound he jabbed it with his finger and drank the sweet liquid until he was sated. And he continued on his way.

It was a hard journey on his knees and soon he was thirsty again. Once more he stumbled upon a mound, pressed it with his finger and drank his fill.

By now it was getting light. But the light bobbed and weaved and blinked so much it made him dizzy. For a third time he came upon a mound and now he could see that it was covered in slender columbines: pressing them between his fingers he drank their sweet juice and went on. The light seemed to bob and blink even more as he came to a plain: as he went farther he saw a great swarm of mosquitoes approaching. It was they who were blocking out the light as they massed in their hundreds and thousands before him.

As soon as they spotted the young man, the mosquito people swarmed towards him, but he quickly caught their leader between his hands and killed him. Then a tiny mosquito said to him:

'Come with us and eat. You must be very hungry.'

The boy accepted the invitation and soon found himself surrounded by a host of humming mosquitos. He was brought a wooden tray piled high with food and told to eat as much as he desired. However, just as he was about to begin, the mosquito people dived into the food; in their greed, the voracious insects riddled the tray with a thousand holes, and the boy only managed to swallow a small portion of the food.

'Rest awhile,' the same tiny mosquito told him, 'before continuing on your way. You have not so far to go now. Should you meet any more of our people, kill the leader as you did just now, and the rest will treat you well.'

The boy took a rest and then set off again. Presently he noticed that the light was once more blinking as if a thousand tiny shadows were blocking out the sun. This time, as he approached, he saw that it was the fly people who were racing towards him. Clapping his hands to squash the leader, he soon heard a trembling voice from amidst the swarm addressing him:

'Pray come and eat with us, you've come a long way and must be hungry.'

He was surrounded on all sides by the fly people who led him to their home and swiftly brought him a trayful of food. As he started to eat, the fly people descended greedily upon the food and soon the tray was gnawed right through, handle and all.

'Rest awhile before you continue your journey,' they urged him. 'By and by you will reach a big settlement. And when you come to the largest yaranga you must halt on the spot where the woman empties the urine and wait there. You will then be told what to do.'

After a short rest, the lad went farther. In a while, it became quite light although the sun was nowhere in sight. He walked on and on until finally he saw a very large yaranga. Making his way quietly towards it, he did not enter; instead, he stood waiting by the tent flap on the spot where the urine was emptied. In no time at all, a woman emerged from the yaranga carrying the echuulgin, the night vessel. As she was about to empty the echuulgin, she caught sight of the young man. Without a word, she cast the urine upon the ground and re-entered the yaranga.

'There is a young man standing outside,' she told the Master of the yaranga.

'Then ask him in,' the Master said.

So the woman went back outside to invite the eighth brother in. Once inside, the Master asked him about himself and his journey.

'There were eight of us brothers,' the lad explained. 'While we were hunting a whale, our canoe was carried out to sea; it drifted very far until we came to the Land of Gloom. One by one my brothers disappeared without a trace. And I have been seeking them ever since, though I remember very little of my journey.'

'Eat now,' ordered the Master. 'You have come far and you must rest. Tomorrow you shall see your family at a thanksgiving feast. All the people of your settlement will be there and you will see them.'

The young man ate and slept soundly until dawn. Then the Master summoned the boy to him.

In the center of the yaranga stood a huge spot. Thrusting it aside, the Master instructed the boy to look below.

And as he gazed curiously down through the hole, he was amazed to see all the family he had left behind; they seemed to be celebrating a festival. The sun was shining brightly upon them and it lit up their happy faces as they ate, sang and danced. So overcome was the young man at this joyful scene that he burst into tears.

'Oh dear, oh dear,' the people below cried, looking up. 'What's this? Rain on such a sunny day . . . Quick, everyone, take the food back into the tents, we'll all be soaked.'

At that the Master of the yaranga addressed the boy:

'That's enough. Stand back while I close the hole, otherwise you'll drench them all with your tears. You may have another look later.'

By and by, after the lad had recovered from seeing all his kinsfolk, he was again invited to look down through the hole.

Thrusting the pot aside, the Master let him look down. All his kinsfolk were there, as if he were in the midst of them. The sun was now shining brightly again and men were tossing their offerings into the air as high as they could; chunks of meat flew high into the sky. The Master snatched up the best pieces and kicked the rest back down again with his foot and they fell to earth.

'So there you are,' said the Master, closing the hole. 'Your kinsmen have now finished offering thanks to me and to the spirits.'

The boy grieved deeply for his family.

Next day, the Master told him:

'I see you miss your kinsfolk. Since that be so, I shall take pity on you and send you home.'

Taking a very long strap, the Master tied one end to the boy's waist and the other to the pot which he had once more pushed aside. Before he lowered the boy through the hole, he spoke these grave words to him:

'I shall allow you to your kinsmen. But mark my words well or you will die: do not enter your parents' home before your mother and father recognize you. When they ask about your brothers, say they are all dead. And let your parents slay your dog in sacrifice to me. Now go.'

Thus the Master instructed the boy and lowered him down on the strap to earth.

Once upon his own dear soil, he stood and waited until his parents emerged from their tent and recognized their long-lost son.

'But where are your seven brothers?' they asked at once.

'They are all dead,' he replied. 'I return alone.'

'Well, you at least remain alive, my son,' his father said. 'We must hurry to offer up a sacrifice so that no more harm befalls you. Mother, bring a reindeer, the leanest!'

'No, you must not offer a reindeer,' said the boy, hurriedly. 'Where is my old dog whom I used to play with? He should be given as an offering to the Great Master. Then all will be well.'

'Certainly not,' insisted his father. 'The dog is our sacred guardian and we have many reindeer. I shall select an old, lean buck; that will suffice.'

No matter how much the boy pleaded with his father, the old man was adamant. He had a reindeer slaughtered and offered up to the kelets. That done, they all entered the yaranga and lay down to sleep: the boy, his mother and his father.

But when the parents awoke the next morning, they found their last son dead.

'Why did we begrudge the dog? they cried, weeping for their youngest son. 'Now we have lost all our children.'

The old folk wept and accused one another. But they never saw their children again.

ANKAKUMIKAITYN THE NOMAD WOLF

One summer the fox heard that Ankakumikaityn the nomad wolf was courting his neighbor, the elder she-dog.

So the wily fox made himself an outfit of wolf's clothing: a gray fur cloak, boots and cap. Then, when the she-dog's brothers were away and she was at home with her younger sister he called upon her.

'I have two herds of fat reindeer,' said the fox to the elder sister, as he sipped the bilberry tea she offered him. 'I have come to seek your hand.'

Thinking that this was, indeed, Ankakumikaityn the nomad wolf, the she-dog treated him to reindeer meat, hot mare's-blood sausages, raw walrus liver and pickled fish, the very choicest pieces. All the while, the fox sat in his cap, unwilling to take it off lest he be recognized.

'Being a wealthy person,' he explained, 'I keep my cap on that people might respect me.'

All of a sudden, the sound of dogs barking could be heard from afar.

'It is my brothers returning from hunting,' the she-dog said.

'Oh dear,' exclaimed the fox, 'they will likely scare my herds. I must run to caution them.'

Once away from the tent, the fox quickly dashed up the nearby hill and loosened some rocks. When the dog brothers came in sight, he pushed the boulders down the hillside and crushed them all. Thereupon, he returned to the yaranga and finished his tea, beguiling the sisters with his oily-tongued tales. As dusk fell and the sisters were busy about their housework, he made off with all their food supplies.

Early next morning, the sisters became most alarmed on discovering their supplies gone and their brothers still absent. As they searched the valley and found their poor brothers dead, they wept in despair.

'Who could have done us such harm?' they wailed.

In their sorrow, they decided to go to Ankakumikaityn to seek his counsel. The nomad wolf was puzzled.

'But I never came to you yesterday!' he exclaimed.

It was not long before the sisters realized they had been tricked by the fox. With the wolf's help, they worked out a plan to get their revenge.

Next day, the fox, unaware that he had been discovered called on the sisters again dressed as Ankakumikaityn. But this time they were expecting him. While the fox drank bilberry tea and exchanged pleasantries, the nomad wolf stealthily entered the yaranga, grabbed the treacherous fox and tied him up.

'What shall we do with the scoundrel?' asked the wolf.

'Let's put him in a sack and leave him in the tundra,' suggested the two sisters.

That they did. The poor fox almost fainted from fright, wondering what his fate would be. At last, he was set down with a bump; the younger sister collected a heap of dry grass and brushwood for a fire, piled it round the sack, surrounded the tinder with stones and then lit the fire.

Poor fox. He at last burst out of the burning sack, his wolf's clothing aflame, and rushed headlong over the tundra like a burning torch.

Satisfied at their revenge, the dog sisters and the wolf returned to the yaranga. Ankakumikaityn wed the elder sister, and the younger dog looked after their children. Some time later, she found herself a husband too.

Since that time red foxes began to appear in the tundra. So it seems that wily old fox, scorched and fiery red, managed to survive his roasting after all.

NET-POS-HU THE ARCHER

At the time of the first creation, there dwelt in a walrus-skin choom on Seal Island a man and his wife, solitary and childless. To all winds their island was surrounded by water with no land in sight.

They lived there more years than they could recall, grieving to one another:

'And so, it seems, we shall end our days on this wretched island, never hearing another human voice.'

But, then, one day a son was born to them, a fine lad, sturdy and handsome.

No name came readily to mind for the newborn boy until one day the old man saw the boy lying on a reindeer skin gazing at an ancient hunting bow on the wall. Taking this as a long-awaited omen, the father named his son Net-Pos-Hu the Archer.

Little Archer began to grow even faster than the wiry spring grass. Soon he was big and strong, a real hunter. It was not long before he had explored the entire island, getting to know every tree and shrub and stone. Nothing fresh remained to be found, and he began to feel bored.

'Is there land yonder?' he asked his father one day.

'There is, my son, though very, very far, way beyond the sea.'

'And do people live there?'

'Yes, there are people, too, many people.'

Soon after this, the son resolved to go in search of other humans, to hear the sound of laughter of the young. His parents begged him not to go.

'Do not leave us; you have all the fish you need.'

'But I want more than food,' he replied.

His parents begged him again and again.

134

'Then wait until your arms and legs are stronger.'

'Even so, I have much strength,' said the young man.

'What if you encounter misfortune? The terrible Mengk may catch you in the forest,' they persisted.

But he would not be put off.

'Net-Pos-Hu fears nothing! he exclaimed boldy.

And he set to fashioning himself a strong kayak, sharpened his arrow-heads until they could pierce a stone, bade farewell to his father and mother and set off.

The young archer sailed on and on; the sun climbed steadily across the sky and sank into the sea. Once more it rose and sank again. And the boy's frail craft sailed on through the waves, its helmsman guiding it he knew not where. But no land came into view.

For many, many days and nights he crossed the rough cold sea, ate all his fish provisions and grew weaker and weaker.

At long last, to his great joy, he sighted a cluster of tall larches on the horizon waving their plumy crests against the sky. Paddling on with renewed strength he finally reached land. And as he glanced ashore he was surprised to see the land knew no bounds. As far as the eye could see there were land and trees and shrubs.

Boldly the young man made his way ashore and came to an aspen grove: in the centre stood a huge aspen whose girth was such as to take four men to encircle it. Its roots twisted and knotted above the soil like some giant's gnarled fingers. Was this the home of the fearful Mengk?

Drawing back his bowstring, Net-Pos-Hu let fly an arrow straight at the base of the tree, just below its roots, wondering what sort of beast would spring out to attack him – a weasel, wolverine, sable or fox?

To his amazement it was a little old woman who emerged from under the roots, shaking her puny fists at him.

'What's the meaning of this?' she screamed. 'Why do you shoot an arrow into my home?'

The young archer explained that he had arrived from a distant island across the sea and did not know the ways of the people.

'I fired into your home without evil intent. How could I know that people in these parts dwell under the roots of an aspen?'

'We live this way because of Mengk, the Evil One,' said the old woman. 'He won't let people catch fish or hunt game; they have to scratch a living where they can.'

'Then I shall destroy the Evil One,' the lad replied, 'so that all may live in peace.'

'Boldly spoken,' said the old woman. 'But you cannot do that without my help.'

With that she dodged back under the aspen roots and soon re-emerged bringing with her a mouse's skin with tiny feet and teeth, a raven's skin with beak and claws, a knife and an iron arrow.

'Put on this mouse's skin and you will turn into a mouse. Put on the raven's skin and you will at once turn into a raven. Loose my arrow and you will never miss your mark; and my knife will never become dull nor bend. Now you are prepared.'

Thanking the old woman, Net-Pos-Hu set off in the direction she showed him. As he made his way through the silent forest, he noticed that no birds sat on the branches of the trees, not a trace of wild animals was to be found over all the land.

Where had all the birds and the beasts gone?

On he walked until he could walk no farther; for across his path stretched an iron net strung from the ground right up to the sky. Straightaway he put on his mouse's skin and squeezed under the mesh. Then, taking human shape again, he proceeded farther.

By and by he arrived in those parts where the Evil One had his dwelling. Climbing a tall larch, Net-Pos-Hu perched on a stout branch and peered to all sides.

And there he was – Mengk, the Evil One – stretched out on the ground. If he were to stand up his head would surely reach beyond the tallest cedar! As the young archer looked and wondered, the giant raised his ugly head and gazed to the south. Net-Pos-Hu followed his gaze and saw a large flock of birds flying that way. The giant lifted his hand, put it to his mouth and blew, thereby enveloping the birds in a fierce gust of wind. They scattered in confusion and flew straight back the way they had come.

'What now?' wondered Net-Pos-Hu.

He did not have long to wait, for soon a score of animals ventured into view. Fine beasts they were: elk and bear, fox and sable, marten and squirrel. Mengk spied them at once, raised his foot and stamped upon the ground, creating such a din and dust that the animals all turned and fled.

'Small wonder the hunters hereabouts never see any game!' the lad mused. 'They'll surely die of hunger unless Mengk is slain.'

He fitted the sharpest arrow to his bow and let fly at the giant, hitting him below his right ear. Mengk let out a roar of pain, tore the tiny arrow from his neck and immediately spotted the boy as he swung round sharply. Net-Pos-Hu would certainly have been snatched from the larch tree had he not quickly donned the raven's skin and flown high above the giant.

Mengk leaped up in pursuit, waving his arms and blowing hard. A black storm blew up, knocking all the cones from the cedars and bending all the trees. Meanwhile, the raven flew on towards the iron net, soared up and over it, higher than the clouds themselves. Just behind him, Mengk thundered on, cleared the net in a single bound and landed with a thud on the other side.

Net-Pos-Hu now took his former shape and hid behind a tree: quickly he set an arrow in his bow – the one given him by the old woman – took aim and fired it straight at Menk's heart.

What a fearful roar the giant let out! He fell to the ground, rolled over and over, beating his arms upon the soil, then lay quite still.

The young archer began to summon the people.

'Mengk is no more,' he announced. 'Now no one will prevent you from hunting and fishing.'

And handing them the old woman's knife, he said:

'Take this sharp knife and cut down the iron net.'

The people cut down the net, hacking it into tiny pieces. To their surprise the knife remained unbent and as sharp as before.

From that time on everyone lived well: there were fish in plenty in the streams and the sea, and game was plentiful in the forests, enough for all the people.

Nor did Net-Pos-Hu want for anything. He remained among the people, fishing and hunting, and rejoiced in their laughter and their games. After a time he took a wife and returned no more to his childhood home on the lonely island across the sea.

GREEDY MOGUS AND THE ORPHANS

There was once a boy and a girl: the boy was certainly larger than a man's thumb though smaller than a giant; the girl was just like any other girl. And the two were orphans.

One time, as they were playing in the yard before their yurta home with their only calf, Greedy Mogus appeared from out of nowhere. What a terrible ogre he was to be sure! With a single bloodshot eye in the center of his forehead and a crooked tusk at the corner of his mouth, he could frighten folk to death just by staring at them.

'Ah ha!' he roared. 'How hungry I am! Now I shall smack my lips and grind my teeth on some juicy children.'

He shouted so loudly that his voice echoed thrice around the distant forest.

'Come here, little ones, and climb into my sack. Be quick about it.'

'But we are only skin and bone,' cried the boy. 'Let us kill our calf and eat it first, then we shall be plump and tasty. Come back and eat us later.'

'A good idea,' rumbled Greedy Mogus. 'I'll be back in ten days. So be it, my little ones, so be it.'

For nine days the children fatted up their calf; and on the tenth day they rose early and, though it pained them greatly, they slew their only calf. Then they cut out his entrails and spread them across the entrance to the yurta. Next they concealed a crane's egg in the hot cinders of the hearth, dropped a live pike into a water barrel, hammered nails upwards through a bench and covered it with a cloth. And under the tree growing in the yard they put a big pile of stones. That done, they skinned

139

the calf and took the hide with them as they climbed into the topmost branches of the tree.

Towards midday, Greedy Mogus came stumping towards the yurta. However, as he crossed the threshold his huge feet slipped upon the scattered entrails and he fell to the ground with an ear-spitting crash. Cursing and groaning, he tried to pull himself up, stumbled across the floor and sprawled into the cinders, thereby breaking the crane's egg and burning his fingers.

'Ooohh, aaahh! Those two-eyed devils!' he roared. 'What have they done to me?' And he thrust his smarting hands into the barrel of water: at once the pike's sharp teeth bit into his fingers. Greedy Mogus let out a howl of range and pain and fell back on to the bench where the nails pierced his seat and he sprang up roaring:

'Aaarrh! You two-legged, two-eyed devils! Where are you? Let me get at you.'

'Yoo-hoo!' called the children, from the top of the tree.

'So there you are! Now I've got you!' Mogus screamed.

And he quickly clambered up the tree after the children. When he was half-way up, the children dropped the calf's hide over his head. Unable to see, he thought it was one of the orphans who had fallen and tried to seize him; but he lost his grip, crashed down from the tree on to the pile of stones and broke his neck.

And that was the end of Greedy Mogus.

LITTLE OONYANI

There were many Evenk people once living peacefully in the taiga. They were happy, contented folk who, when their fishing and hunting were done, would sing and dance and play their games in the quiet of the northern evening.

And then one day an evil came upon them: a great whirring was heard in the sky above the taiga and when the people looked up they saw to their horror a strange terrible figure flying overhead.

It was the evil shaman and man-eater, Korendo.

Whenever Korendo was hungry he would put on his wings, fly wherever he wished and eat men and women, even little children.

Korendo now flew down among the chooms and began to seize the people: nobody could escape him, he caught them all and every one – and gobbled them up in an instant.

Every living creature was devoured by the evil Korendo; all but one old woman who sat very still under an upturned iron pot, hoping he would not find her. And he did not. Thinking he had eaten the entire settlement, he waved his wings, rose higher and higher into the clouds and flew away towards the setting sun.

When the whirring had passed, the old woman crawled out from under the iron pot and went to seek her kin: not a soul remained. The lonely woman burst into tears.

'How shall I live all by myself?' she cried.

Peering into every choom, she found them empty, all except the last one. And there to her great joy she found a baby lying in the corner. She made a cradle to rock him in, cared for him and watched him grow.

And she called the child Oonyani – the Lonely One.

The little boy seemed to grow more by the hour than by the

141

day; and when he was soon full-grown he went hunting and fed the old woman with reindeer meat. One day he asked her:

'Grannie, why are only you and I living here? Where are all our people? Did they die?'

'It happened all in one night, my son,' she replied. 'They were eaten by Korendo the man-eater, save you and me. I hid under an iron pot and you were so small the monster didn't see you. I found you and brought you up.'

The young man grew very angry.

'What became of that man-eater? I shall kill him!'

'I would surely tell you if I knew,' she replied.

Oonyani was determined to find Korendo and punish him. So he went into the taiga, caught a wild deer and brought it to the choom.

'Grannie,' he said, 'is this the one who slew our people?'

'No, my son, that is not the one. That is deer, a gentle creature. Take him back into the forest and free him.'

Oonyani took back the wild deer and let him go; then he went farther into the forest and caught a wolverine, dragging it back to the choom to show his grandmother.

'Grannie,' he said, 'is this the one who slew our people?'

'No, no, my son,' she replied. 'That is wolverine; he is not guilty of anything. Take him back and let him go.'

Oonyani obeyed the old woman and let the wolverine go. Next he caught a caribou and took it back to the choom.

'Grannie, is this the one who ate our people?'

'No, my son,' she said, 'he is not guilty. That is caribou. He doesn't eat people. Take him back and set him free.'

Oonyani let the caribou go and then caught a wolf.

'Grannie, is this the one who ate our people?'

'No, no, my son. That is wolf. Let him go.'

So Oonyani freed the wolf and caught a bear. And the old woman told him to let bear go too. And so it was Oonyani brought back all the animals, big and small. But all of them had to be set free again.

Poor Oonyani could not understand: not knowing what to do and whom to punish, he grew very miserable. At last the old woman could bear his gloomy mood no longer and told him this:

'Do not search for the man-eater in the taiga. He flew to us on wings like a bird and came from out of the sky. Where he went I do not know. All I know is that he is called Korendo.'

No more did Oonyani go into the taiga. He asked the old woman for the lid of an iron pot, took a hammer and set to making himself a pair of wings. All day long he sat at the fire forging the great wings; and when he was through he asked the old woman whether the wings would do.

'No, my son,' she said, 'they won't do: Korendo's wings were bigger.'

Once again Oonyani set about his task, making his wings bigger. When he had finished he wanted to try them out, so he flew up into the sky and called down to the old woman:

'Grannie, did Korendo fly as high as a black grouse?'

'Even higher.'

Again Oonyani set to forging a pair of wings. He made them even bigger than the last, put them on and flew up once more, calling down:

'Grannie, did Korendo fly as high as a hazel grouse?'

'Even higher. To overcome him you must fly even higher than he can. Remember, Korendo is very big and strong.'

Oonyani set to work with a will, sat at the fire without a rest, hammering away at his wings until he had forged himself another pair of strong iron wings. When they were ready he put them on and rose into the sky to try them out. As he soared through the air, he shouted down:

'Grannie, tell me, did Korendo fly higher than me?'

'No, my son. Now you are flying higher than Korendo.'

Oonyani soared up to a great height, rose even into the clouds and saw an enormous choom in the distance. And he flew toward it.

When he arrived at the monster's dwelling, he began to circle above it singing out loudly:

>*'Come out, come out, Korendo,*
>*I come to take revenge on you!'*

Over and over he sang the same words, but Korendo did not emerge from the choom. He was not at home. Instead, his wife appeared and sang out to him:

> *'Oh, how silly you are*
> *To come here all alone,*
> *To pit your strength against Korendo!*
> *He is a mighty shaman*
> *Whom no one can defeat.'*

With a shake of his wings, Oonyani flew on far across the taiga. Finally he came to a second huge choom where Korendo had his dwelling. Circling above it, Oonyani began to summon him:

> *'Come out, come out, Korendo,*
> *I come to take revenge on you!'*

But instead of Korendo, his second wife came out of the choom and sang him a reply:

> *'Korendo is a mighty shaman*
> *Whom no one can defeat;*
> *If you wish to die*
> *To Korendo now fly!'*

She sang her song and showed Oonyani the way farther. On and on he flew until he spotted a third great choom in the distance. As he flew up, he called out his challenge to Korendo. But again he was not at home. On flew Oonyani to a fourth choom, yet Korendo was not there either. Nor was he at home in the fifth or the sixth, but he learned from Korendo's sixth wife that the man-eater was now living in the seventh choom. And all Korendo's wives with whom Oonyani had spoken sang him the same song:

> *'Korendo is a mighty shaman*
> *Whom no one can defeat;*
> *If you wish to die*
> *To Korendo now fly!'*

Yet their words did not scare Oonyani. On he flew to the seventh choom and as he arrived he circled overhead, singing:

> *'Come out, come out, Korendo,*
> *I come to take revenge on you!'*

Oonyani's singing came to the ears of Korendo's seventh wife who came out of the choom to sing him a reply:

> *'Do not wake the fearsome ogre*
> *Lest he eat you bones and all*
> *He will surely fly above you,*
> *Catch and swallow one so small.'*

Her words did not frighten Oonyani; he began to circle lower and lower, singing more and more loudly:

> *'Korendo slew all my people,*
> *Now I come to take revenge.*
> *Though I am small, I fear him not*
> *Let him know that I am here.'*

Korendo's wife disappeared into the choom to wake the man-eater, then returned to sing out a reply to Oonyani:

> *'Mighty Korendo has woken*
> *And is putting on his wings.*
> *In a moment he will kill you*
> *Death and destruction he now brings.'*

Oonyani flew right above Korendo's choom, bravely shouting his challenge:

> *'Korendo, Korendo, Korendo!*
> *Come out and fight me now.'*

The terrible roar of the man-eater came bursting out of the choom:

> *'Oonyani, Oonyani, Oonyani!*
> *Just you wait, just you wait*
> *While I eat and drink my fill.'*

145

But Oonyani sang even louder:

> *'Why do you eat, Korendo?*
> *You haven't long to live.'*

Korendo's hoarse voice was now raised in fury:

> *'Oonyani, Oonyani, Oonyani!*
> *Just wait while I pull on my boots.'*

And little Oonyani sang back:

> *'Why pull on your boots, Korendo?*
> *You've not long to live this life.'*

Korendo roared back:

> *'Oonyani, Oonyani, Oonyani!*
> *Just wait while I put on my wings.'*

But Oonyani would not leave the monster in peace, and he sang out his challenge once more:

> *'Korendo, Korendo, Korendo!*
> *Why do you dally in your choom?*
> *Scared you are to face me,*
> *Afraid to face your doom.'*

At that the man-eater rushed from the choom and threw himself at little Oonyani. But the agile boy flew swiftly and easily into the air. With an angry flapping of his wings, Korendo tried to fly higher than Oonyani, yet the boy kept above his head just out of reach.

On and on they flew, higher and higher, with Oonyani keeping just above the evil shaman who flailed and flapped his wings, desperate to get at his young tormentor. After a while, Korendo became weary from his exertions and sang out:

> *'My head's in a spin,*
> *My lungs are fit to burst.*
> *Come down to the plain*
> *And I'll grind you to dust.'*

146

Oonyani gave a triumphant laugh:

> *'So, your head's in a spin*
> *And your lungs are fit to burst.*
> *Then remember my kin*
> *Whom you slaughtered first.'*

With that, Oonyani dived down to Korendo and flew round and round his head, singing loudly:

> *'Korendo, Korendo, Korendo!*
> *No more will you leave our homes bare.*
> *No more will you put out our fire,*
> *Never again will you fly through the air.*
> *It is time to ascend from your pyre.'*

And he landed on Korendo's back and snapped off one wing. At once the huge monster plunged down like a stone, struck the ground with a great crash and split asunder from end to end. And out of his broken belly spilled all the people he had ever swallowed – alive and unharmed. All of them followed the brave Oonyani back to their chooms, once more to live in peace and calm.

As for the broken man-eater shaman, his seven wives gathered up his remains and burned them, his soul ascending to the upper world amid the smoke of his own funeral pyre.

THE WATER SPRITE

Long, long ago in a deep lake there lived a water sprite who guarded the lake from the forest people. One day he saw a man of the Tofalar clan laying his nets in the lake.

'Why do you do that?' asked the sprite.

'So as to catch fish,' the man replied.

Now, the water sprite did not wish to give up his fish, so he challenged the man to a contest.

The two came to grips but the puny water sprite was no match for the sturdy fisherman, and the man quickly got the better of him.

'I'll take my revenge tomorrow,' warned the sprite.

'Not from me, you won't,' answered the man. 'You're not strong enough for me; you'll have to take on my younger brother.'

It so happened that the younger brother was a bear, and it was he who would next fight the quarrelsome sprite. Next day, as the bear was picking some berries, the sprite crept up behind and pounced on him. They grappled together for some moments, but the bear, like the fisherman before, was too strong for the sprite and threw him on his back.

But that water sprite would not give in so easily. Next day, just to show what he could do, he flung his whip into the sky beyond the clouds. The fisherman followed the whip with a sneer.

'That's nothing,' he said. 'I can fling this willow stick even higher.'

And he drew back his arm as if to toss it high, but instead dropped it quietly over his shoulder; with his head in the air, the sprite noticed nothing amiss and thought the man had made good his boast.

'It is evident that Tofalar men are stronger than I am,' he said, at last. 'And quicker too. I shall quarrel with you no more. You may come down from the hills and catch as many fish as you like; I shall stay in the depths and not show myself to you again.'

And so it was. It is very rare indeed these days for a man to meet a water sprite.

WHY THE SUN FORSOOK THE TUNDRA

One day long ago, the Sun sent his sister the Moon down to earth to gather some berries. She glided gracefully through the sky, landed lightly on a bed of moss and walked over the tundra. She had not gone far when she met Mistress Crow and at once they made friends. Together, the Moon and the Crow collected berries until their baskets were full.

Since the task was uncommon to the Moon, she soon felt tired; so she lay down on a stretch of grass and was shortly fast asleep. As she slumbered, her companion gazed at her pale and delicate countenance and was amazed at her beauty.

'What a lovely bride she would make for my brother,' breathed Mistress Crow.

As dusk was falling, the Moon awoke and the two friends made their way for shelter to the Crow's yaranga. And there the Crow's brother was immediately captivated by the pale incandescent Moon.

'See how lovely the Moon Maiden is,' whispered his sister. 'She would make you a worthy wife. Listen, I have a plan: when she goes berrying in the tundra tomorrow, you accompany her dressed as me.'

Young Master Crow rose early next morning, put on his sister's brown dress and wakened Mistress Moon. They partook of some reindeer meat, drank tea and set off to look for berries.

But while Moon was about her task, she again felt tired and soon lay down to take a rest. When at last she awoke, there was no sign of her companion. Instead she found a handsome hunting knife by her side. Concealing it in the folds of her dress, Mistress

Moon decided it was time to return to her brother the Sun. With her basket of berries and hunting knife, she therefore flew up to the sky. But as she flew through the air, she felt the knife slip from her and fall towards the earth. How surprised she was to see it turn into the crow brother of her first companion!

Master Crow steadied himself and flew up in pursuit of the fleeing Moon.

'You cannot fly with me to the Sun,' called the Moon. 'You will be scorched and will shrivel to nothing.'

Master Crow declared his love.

'I cannot leave you, O my beloved Moon,' he moaned. 'I'll fly with you just as long as my strength lasts; and then I shall fall to the cruel rocks below. I cannot live without you.'

Poor Mistress Moon took pity on the Crow and returned to earth with him. They began to live together and it was not long before a child was born.

In the meantime, the Sun was waiting impatiently for his sister; all the Sun's children, the little sunbeams, were singing mournful songs of the young maiden who had lost her way on earth. But there was no sign of Mistress Moon. At last, the Sun descended to earth himself and lit up the entire tundra with his rays – all the mountain caverns, the deep ravines and the fast-flowing rivers – until all was as clear as crystal. It was not long before one of the Sun's rays fell upon his sister the Moon, sitting within the Crow's yaranga.

At once the Sun flew there, peeped behind its felt curtain and discovered that his long-lost sister.

'Why did you stay so long on earth, my sister?' he asked.

'I know I have wronged you, my brother,' answered the Moon. 'But I could not leave my husband and my earth-child.'

At that the Sun grew angry and set upon the Crow.

'Moon is my only sister; her place is in the sky. She must return to me at once.'

'But Moon is also my wife,' objected the Crow. 'And she has my child.'

The Sun and the Crow argued long about who was to have the Moon. And finally it was decided to settle the question in a contest: each would nominate a sewing-woman and the one who could sew a suit of clothes faster would be the victor.

The Crow summoned Mistress Ermine, while the Sun called Mistress Mouse. Each received a reindeer skin and was ordered to sew a fur robe from it. In no time at all, Mistress Ermine had made a most delightful robe, while Mistress Mouse had hardly begun.

Next Crow chose Mistress Marmot, and the Sun chose Mistress Gopher. And they began to sew fur trousers. In no time at all, Mistress Marmot had finished a handsome pair of fur trousers, while Mistress Gopher had not done half the job.

Then the Crow summoned Mistress Otter, and the Sun called Mistress Fox. They were to sew fur stockings. Once again, the Crow's choice won. Then it was the turn of Mistress Bear against Mistress Wolf; in no time at all the nimble Mistress Bear had made a splendid pair of fur boots, leaving Mistress Wolf far behind. The Crow had won again. After that, he summoned Mistress Goat, while the Sun called Mistress Lynx to sew a pair of mittens. Once again the contest began and the Goat made a fine pair of mittens in record time, long before the Lynx had completed just one.

Seeing that he was losing the contest, the Sun sent his rays to fetch the beautiful Ice Maiden to the Crow's yaranga. Caught in the rays of the Sun, Ice Maiden's countenance gleamed and sparkled brilliantly, blinding the Crow with her beauty.

'Give me back my sister,' said the Sun, 'and you shall have the lovely Ice Maiden for your wife.'

The Crow was sorely tempted, but he replied:

'No, I shall not. No maiden can compare with the lovely Moon.'

Then the Sun sent his rays after the Snow Maiden and had her brought to him. As she entered the yaranga enveloped in the bright rays of the Sun, the Snow Maiden sparkled with many fires and the yaranga at once shone brightly.

The Crow's greed got the better of him at last.

'Take your sister and leave me these two lovely maidens!' he said, finally.

Together with the Moon and her child, the Sun returned to the heavens, leaving Master Crow in the company of the lovely Ice Maiden and the lovely Snow Maiden. But they no longer dazzled and gleamed without the brilliant rays of the Sun.

And the Sun, cross with the Crow for parting so easily with his beautiful sister, departed for lands far away to the south. And ever since the long, long winter has been cold and dark throughout the tundra.

MAYAKI

There was once a man named Canda who had two wives: one his favorite Ayaula, the other Gayula. Ayaula dwelt with her husband in one yurta, while Gayula lived alone in a straw hut doing all the chores: she sewed, cooked and fed the dogs. All Ayaula had to do was comb her husband's hair and eat.

Two children were born to Canda: Ayaula bore him a girl who was named Gandusa, while Gayula bore him a boy, Mayaki. Poor Gayula had to feed both the babies.

With the passing of time, the children took shape and form: Gandusa was a cry-baby and very lazy, while Mayaki was fearless; he would run about the taiga and along the riverbank, he assisted his mother in her chores and shot squirrels with his bow.

One day Mayaki accidentally pushed his sister over; and she bumped her nose, burst into tears and quickly ran to tell their father. At once Canda and his favorite Ayaula came running up, railed at Gayula that she had taught her son rough ways and, while Ayaula beat her with a stick, Canda took a forked twig and poked out her eyes.

'With those eyes you should have watched out, now you will see nothing!' he hissed. And he threw the eyes into the stream.

Gayula remained blind. Now it was Mayaki's turn to feed his mother, killing birds and squirrels and bringing them home to cook on the fire. And so he grew up. One day, his sister Gandusa came running to see how they were faring, and Mayaki told her:

'You've no doubt come to see if we're still alive?'

And he drove her away, so that she again ran off to her father to tell tales. When she had gone, Mayaki left the hut, tapped himself lightly on the head with a stick and turned into a bird.

154

Flying to his father's yurta, he alighted on the crossbeam of the smoke-hole and began to listen to what was being said inside. As soon as Gandusa came in, she complained that Mayaki had beaten her. Her father flew into a rage.

'If Mayaki is so strong, why does he not go in search of his mother's eyes? Should he find them, he can really boast that he is strong.'

Hearing these words, Mayaki flew back to the straw hut, took on his proper form and told his mother:

'Mother, let us make a birch-bark canoe, I shall cross the sea in it to seek your eyes.'

'But your father only wishes to have you killed, my son,' she said. 'You are too small to sail so far. I can live without my eyes.'

But Mayaki would not be dissuaded. So together mother and son made a birch-bark canoe and Mayaki put to sea. He rowed and rowed and his tiny craft bobbed up and down on the waves like a wood-shaving. All the same, he crossed the sea safely and came to a strange shore where two young girls were playing, tossing two black eyes to one another across a fire.

'What are you doing?' asked Mayaki.

'We found these two lovely black stones on the shore and we are playing a catching game with them,' the girls replied.

Mayaki joined in the game, his heart pounding. But not for a moment did he forget why he had come. After they had been playing for a while, both the little stones landed in Mayaki's hands. Quickly, he thrust them into his pouch and ran down to the sea before the girls could stop him. He jumped into his canoe and rowed off as hard as he could. On and on he rowed until he eventually arrived at his own shore. Straightaway he rushed to his mother and returned to her the two eyes. Once again his mother was able to see. And she was very happy.

It was not long, of course, before the inquisitive Gandusa again came to see them.

'Have you come to see whether we have died of hunger?' asked Mayaki.

And he drove the girl away. Then he tapped himself lightly on the head with a stick, turned into a bird and flew to his father's yurta; there he settled on the crossbeam of the smokehole and began to listen to the conversation. When Gandusa arrived she told her tales: how Mayaki had found his mother's eyes and Gayula could see once again.

'And Mayaki beat me and drove me away,' she said, in tears.

Canda flew into a rage:

'If he is so strong, let him seek a bride beyond the seven hills. The maid's father demands a bride-price of seven matching fox brushes; nobody has yet found them.'

Hearing these words, Mayaki flew to his own hut, turned back into a young man and told his mother:

'In the morning I shall go to seek seven matching fox brushes as a gift for my bride.'

'Do not go, my son,' his mother said. 'Your father wishes only to send you to your death.'

But Mayaki was stubborn and now quite strong, hardened by the taiga and his last journey across the sea. At first light he gathered up his things and, though his mother cried and tried to hold him back, he went on his way. So fast did he ski over the snow that by sundown he had crossed the seven hills and arrived at the home of the old man Mafass, who lived with his wife and lovely daughter Biala. The maid had a pale, round face and hair as black as a raven's wing, and she was wearing a dress that was daintily embroidered by her own fair hands.

Old Mafass questioned the young man:

'Mayaki, why have you come to our dwelling like a fleet-footed stag?'

'Old man, I have come to ask you for your daughter, I wish to marry her.'

Mafass replied firmly:

'I love my daughter and have brought her up well, therefore I ask a high price for her: seven matching fox brushes. Should you find them my daughter shall be your wife at once.'

Now Biala had seen and heard Mayaki, and her heart sang sweetly; it told her that she loved him deeply. So she put a patchwork cloak on him that she had made herself.

'You must cross seven rivers and hills,' she told him, 'before you come to a fox trail. Stand to one side and wait until the foxes come. Among them will be a fox with eight tails; he is the one you want. Hurry, for they pass along the trail only at midday.'

Mayaki pulled on his skis and set off like the wind, sending the snow flurrying behind him. He crossed another seven hills, forded seven rivers and finally came to the fox trail. And there he stood to one side like a dead tree-stump, not moving for fear of frightening the animals. Shortly, a fox with one tail came running up, saw Mayaki standing at the wayside and exclaimed in wonderment:

> *'What is this strange tree-stump by our track?*
> *At daylight I passed and did not notice it,*
> *I passed little streams,*
> *Crossed rivers, large and small,*
> *Yet such a stump all dressed so fine,*
> *I've never set eyes on before.'*

And she ran on by.

Next to come past was a fox with two tails; she saw Mayaki at the wayside and was much amazed:

> *'What is this strange tree-stump by our track?*
> *At daylight I passed and did not notice it.*
> *I passed little streams,*
> *Crossed rivers, large and small,*
> *Yet such a stump all dressed so fine,*
> *I've never set eyes on before.'*

And on she ran past Mayaki.

Thus it was that foxes with three, with four, with five, with six and with seven tails ran past. They passed him by and all stopped in surprise. But Mayaki stood as still as a tree-stump waiting for the fox with eight tails. After some time, that fox came running along proudly waving his eight brushes in the air. They were big and furry, and all a bright rusty brown. When the fox spotted Mayaki standing at the wayside, he stopped and exclaimed:

'What is this strange tree-stump by our track?
At daylight I passed and did not notice it.
I passed little streams,
Crossed rivers, large and small,
Yet such a stump all dressed so fine,
I've never set eyes on before.'

Like an arrow, Mayaki swiftly flew at the fox and, with one blow of his hunting knife, cut off seven of his tails. The fox was caught unawares.

'How is it my brothers did not notice? Why did they not protect me?' the fox said. 'Mayaki, you outwitted my brothers and sisters.'

From that time, all foxes have remained with one brush and they keep out of people's way, sly and cunning for fear that someone will outwit them again.

Mayaki tightly tied to his waist the seven matching fox tails and set off on his return journey. At sundown, he arrived at the home of Mafass, handed over his prize and took the lovely Biala. Then he returned to his mother with his bride.

It was not long, of course, before his sister Gandusa came running to look.

'Have you come to see whether Mayaki is alive or not?' asked Gayula.

As soon as Gandusa saw Mayaki's lovely bride, she ran back to her own home to tell her tales. Meanwhile, Mayaki flew off as before in the shape of a bird to his father's yurta.

As soon as Gandusa came running in, she told how Mayaki's bride had a round, pale face and hair as black as a raven's wing; how her gown was embroidered in pretty patterns by her own fair hands. The father grew envious and desired the young girl for himself. Once more he began to talk of new tasks for the boy:

'Beyond the seven hills, beyond the seven marshes there is a tree whose bark is covered with the scales of serpent skins, whose leaves are of silver and gold, and whose blossoms ring like bells in the wind. If Mayaki really is strong, let him bring us this tree and plant it by our yurta so that we can admire it.'

Hearing this, Mayaki flew back to his hut, took human form and then told his mother and wife:

'I am going in search of a tree beyond the seven hills and seven marshes; its bark is covered with the scales of serpent skins, its leaves are of silver and gold, and its blossoms ring like bells in the wind. My father would have me bring him back this tree.'

His mother begged him not to go, but there was no turning the bold young hunter aside from his dangerous task. At dawn he pulled on his skis and went off in a cloud of swirling snowflakes. He passed over seven hills and seven marshes and at last arrived at a great and murky swamp; there he found the tree he sought standing in the middle of the swamp.

As Mayaki picked his way carefully towards the tree, a strong wind blew up almost knocking him off his feet. So fiercely did it blow that day was turned into night. Yet Mayaki did not falter: he pressed on into the blizzard until he reached the tree. Then it suddenly grew light, the wind dropped and the sun appeared above the tall and marvelous tree. Mayaki summoned up all his strength, put both arms round the tree and pulled it up together with its roots. Then, swinging it seven times round his head, he said:

'Great and wondrous tree, fly to our straw hut and grow as before.'

So saying, he tossed the tree high into the air. It flew so fast its bells rang out like thunder over the taiga; and it struck the ground so hard sparks flew up like lightning.

When Mayaki returned to his hut, there was the tree growing as splendidly as before.

'This night there will be a fierce storm,' he told Biala and his mother. 'Do not be afraid, for I shall protect you.'

And indeed, that night a fierce storm did burst upon the taiga: trees fell, hills crumbled and waves crashed upon the shore. Gayula and Biala were afraid their straw hut would be blown away, but Mayaki slept on soundly.

By morning the wind had abated and the sun was shining. When Mayaki led his mother and wife from their hut, however, they did not recognize the land about them: all had been swept away, including the wonderful tree with leaves of silver and gold. Even Canda's yurta was gone: no Canda, nor his wife Ayaula, nor their daughter Gandusa.

All that remained was Mayaki's straw hut; and by its side grew just two young trees: a little poplar and a slender silver birch. From that time on, the three Udegeis lived in peace: the bold Mayaki, his black-eyed mother and the lovely Biala.

HOW THE SUN WAS RESCUED

Thus it was.

Once upon a time, the tungaks stole the Sun from the tundra dwellers. And in the everlasting gloom that followed all the birds and beasts stumbled about seeking their food by touch.

Soon the birds and the beasts decided to call a grand council; envoys were dispatched to the council from every species of animal and bird.

The old raven whom all considered wise spoke up:

'My friends, how much longer must we dwell in darkness? I have heard that close to our land, in a great cavern, live the tungaks who have stolen the Sun. They keep it in a white stone pot. If we steal back the Sun from the tungaks we can light up our world again. So I, old raven, advise you to send the biggest and strongest among you, the big Polar bear, to fetch the Sun.'

'The bear, the bear!' cried all the animals.

At that moment, the ancient, half-deaf owl was busy repairing her sledge and noticed all the commotion. Asking the little snow bunting nearby for news, she was told that the Polar bear was to be sent to fetch the Sun.

'Oh, no, no, no!' cried the owl. 'That won't do at all. No sooner will he come upon some scrap of food than he'll forget all about his mission. And we'll never get the Sun back.'

With that they all had to agree:

'True enough, the bear will find some scrap of food and forget about everything else.'

The raven spoke again:

'Then let's send the wolf; after the bear he is the strongest and he is much faster.'

161

'Eh, what's that they're saying?' the owl asked the snow bunting.

'They've decided on the wolf,' replied the bunting. 'He is the strongest and swiftest of us all after the bear.'

'Fiddlesticks!' snapped the owl. 'That wolf is greedy and will stop at the first deer he sees and gobble it up; and he'll forget all about the Sun.'

Hearing the owl's words, the animals had to agree.

'Quite true, quite true,' they said. 'That wolf is greedy and when he sees a deer he will stop to kill it, and forget about the Sun. But whom shall we send for the sun?'

Just then a tiny mouse raised her squeaky voice:

'We should send the hare; he's the best runner among us; he'll fetch the Sun back for us.'

Once more the birds and beasts cried out:

'The hare, the hare, the hare!'

And for the third time the deaf old owl asked the snow bunting what they were saying. Back came the answer:

'They want to send the hare for the Sun, for he is the best runner and he may catch the Sun on his way.'

The owl thought for a bit, then said:

'Yes, he may indeed steal back the Sun. He hops well and skips well, and is not selfish. Nobody will be able to catch him.'

So the hare was chosen. Without more ado, he went on his way guided by the raven. He hopped and skipped for many days across the land until at last he spied a shaft of light far ahead.

As he came closer he saw that rays of light were coming from under the earth through a narrow crack. When he put his eye to the crack he was able to make out a ball of fire lying in a great white stone pot, its rays lighting up a vast underground cavern.

'That must be the Sun,' thought the hare. 'And over there must be the tungaks, lying on those soft reindeer hides in the corner.'

The brave little hare squeezed through the crack, let himself down on to the floor of the cavern and hopped over to where the ball of fire lay. Then he snatched it up from the stone pot, banged the ground hard with his hind legs and sprang up through the crack.

At once the tungaks rushed about trying to squeeze through the crack in pursuit of the hare.

In the meantime the little hare ran as fast as his legs would carry him. All the same, it was not long before the speedy tungaks were on his heels. Just as they were about to grab him, he gave the ball of fire a hard kick with his hind legs, breaking it in two: one part small, the other big. With a second kick, he sent the smaller part flying high into the air until it reached the heavens.

And there it became the Moon.

He then kicked the big part even higher so that it soared into another region of the sky to become the Sun.

How bright it then became on earth.

The tungaks were blinded by the light and scampered back underground, never to appear on earth again. And all the birds and the beasts praised the brave little hare who had rescued the Sun.

THE CLAYMAN AND THE GOLDEN-ANTLERED ELK

In the season when water dies, an old fisherman made a man out of clay. Mighty pleased with himself, he stood the Clayman outside his door and went to tell his wife.

The old woman was very frightened.

'What have you done, old man?' she cried, aghast. 'That Clayman will surely kill us both.'

And at that moment, just as she feared, they heard a toop-a-toop-toop behind the door and in burst the Clayman. He stared here and there and soon spied the old man in the corner with his wife, crouching under their nets.

The Clayman seized the old pair and ate them both together; arms, legs and nets in one go. He swallowed the lot and went outside.

Walking past the hut were two village girls, one with pails of water, the other with a wooden yoke. And he devoured the pair of them: one together with her pails, the other with her yoke. And he went on his way.

Coming towards him were three old women carrying baskets full of berries; and he ate them all together with their baskets. And he continued on his way.

Next he spotted three fishermen mending their boat. He quickly gobbled up all three, and their boat for good measure, before he went farther.

Along the way he came upon three woodcutters. And he ate them with their axes and a couple of fallen trees. Then on he went.

On and on he strode until he came to a hill on whose crown a young elk was grazing.

Called the Clayman to the elk:

'I am going to eat you.'

The elk shouted down from the hilltop:

'As you will, Clayman. But stand back with your mouth open to receive me; I'll run down the hill and leap straight into your mouth to save you the trouble of coming for me.'

The Clayman chuckled and gurgled with glee.

So there he stood at the base of the hill, his mouth open as wide as he was able, waiting for the elk to come down to him.

Down the hill ran the elk full tilt and butted the Clayman such a blow in the belly that he burst into little pieces. And all that he had swallowed jumped out of him and ran home:

The old man and woman hauling their nets,

The maids with their pails and yoke,

The old women along with their baskets of berries,

The fishermen and their boat,

The woodcutters with their axes and two trees.

And the elk followed behind.

So thankful were the Lopar people that they brought out all their gold and gilded the elk's antlers. From that time on he became known as the Golden-Antlered Elk, Slayer of the Clayman.

EMEMCOOT AND THE FOREST MAIDEN

This is how it was in the home of Coot and his son Ememcoot.

Lazy Coot lay in the yaranga all day long and never ventured out of doors, so that over the days his hair became matted and tangled.

Busy Ememcoot hunted well in the forest every day, killing many birds and beasts. One day, however, when he was out hunting, he heard a most unusual voice singing.

Who could it be that sang so melodiously?

Ememcoot made his way quietly towards the sound and hid in the hollow of a tree beside the path. Unaware of his presence, the singer came walking along the forest path. As she passed the hollow tree Ememcoot sprang out and embraced the beautiful forest maiden.

She did not resist. Instead, she told him:

'Know well that I am a creature of the forest. If you take me into your home, be warned that I shall bring you misfortune.'

At first Ememcoot said nothing. The wife he had chosen was extremely beautiful and his heart ached for her.

'Come,' he said at last. 'We shall go to my home and live together.'

When Ememcoot and the girl entered the yaranga, Coot still lay on his bed; yet as he set eyes on the newcomer, he leaped up, cast his bed out of the tent and did all he could for the guest.

'Where did you come upon so lovely a creature?' he asked his son.

'I found her in the forest,' was all the son replied.

Being desirous of taking her for himself, Coot racked his

166

brains to think of a way of tricking his son. At last, he hit on a plan: he would send Ememcoot hunting in the hills for black bears and he would surely never return alive. Thus, when night fell, he said:

'Ememcoot, let us go hunting bear tomorrow. I know a lair high in the hills.'

So the next day, the two men set out for the hills. And when they were approaching the lair Coot began to tremble from head to toe, as if mightily afraid.

'You go first,' he whispered to his son.

Suspecting nothing, the young huntsman crept cautiously into the mouth of the lair; and as he knelt there peering into the gloom, a hard shove sent him sprawling head over heels into the midst of the bears.

Meanwhile, the evil Coot ran home and lay beside the lovely forest maiden. But she had covered herself in a garment of nettles that badly stung the old man. Up he jumped in a rage.

'Why is your body covered in sharp needles?' he asked.

'And why did you push my husband into the bears' lair?' she asked in reply.

'All the same,' cried Coot angrily, 'you will submit to me. Ememcoot will be in the bears' stomachs by now.'

But he was wrong. The bears, friends of his dear wife, had received Ememcoot well, fed him on bear's flesh and sent him back home unharmed. Presently, he entered his yaranga.

How pleased his wife was to see him; she immediately threw her arms round his neck. Coot, though, was scared and went outside to spend the night alone under the stars.

It was several days before the old man returned. Once again he suggested the two go off together.

'Ememcoot, let us go fishing. I have seen many good fish in the bay. We shall go and catch them.'

Willingly, the innocent Ememcoot went with his father down to the sea. Yet as they came close and were standing on the shore, Coot stole up behind the lad and knocked him into the water.

But he did not drown. The fish welcomed him as their guest, a loach saying:

'Do not harm this land creature. His father wishes to kill him for his beautiful wife. Prepare a meal of tender loaches for him and send him home safe.'

So the young huntsman ate and slept well before returning to his yaranga. Ememcoot was a man slow to anger and quickly forgave his wicked father. Once again, however, the old man went off into the forest to hatch a new plan and did not return for several days.

On his return, he suggested that they go hunting sable in the hills. Ememcoot suspected nothing and willingly accompanied his father. As the two climbed upwards, the old man dropped behind: he knew they were approaching a deep pit that he had dug the day before and concealed along the track. And, all of a sudden, the unwary hunter vanished into the pit as the twigs gave way beneath his feet. At once, the evil Coot set to filling in the pit, placing a stick so that he should know the place when he returned. Then, once again, he hurried back to the forest maiden.

But Ememcoot did not die. All through the days and nights he worked hard to dig himself out of the deep pit. And at last, he crawled out exhausted; after a long rest, he set off for home.

When he reached the yaranga and found Coot, he told him calmly:

'Old man, you could not kill me, no matter how hard you tried: you pushed me into the bears' lair, but the bears received me well. You knocked me into the icy water, but the fishes received me well. You caused me to fall into a pit, but I dug myself out and returned safe and sound. Now I invite you to accompany me into the forest – as I did with you.'

They did not have to travel far. Ememcoot summoned three polar wolves and four black bears, friends of his wife, and ordered them to form a circle round the wicked Coot from which he could not escape. When this was done, Ememcoot gave an order and the beasts tore the old man to pieces.

From that time on Ememcoot and the forest maiden lived in peace and happiness.

TWO BROTHERS

Long ago, when there was no bitter frost to spread its icy fingers
far and wide, green forests grew across the northern lands. And in
those long-forgotten days gentle breezes warmed the earth.

Where the tundra now stands on pillars of ice there lived a
man called Kuul Kihi, the Wild One.

Kuul Kihi and his wife lived in a wooden house on a hilltop
with no other kin throughout the homelands. They were very
lonely, for they had no children; and not a day would pass but
the wife would say to her husband:

'We've been living on this lonely hilltop for nearly twenty
years, and we've never seen a soul. It is extremely dull here. Go,
my husband, and seek our kinsmen.'

Kuul Kihi finally consented and went in search of other folk.
He put together a few belongings and, taking a bow and three
arrows, said to his wife on parting:

'I shall fire an arrow back home each year, so that you may
know that I am alive. And if, after you see the last of my arrows,
a year passes with no sign from me, you will know that I am
dead. Then you should leave this place and seek other folk to
take you in; but mind you take another track to the one I take
today.'

With these words, Kuul Kihi set off towards the rising sun. He
could not know how much time passed while he was on his way;
when the sun shone it was surely summer, and when the trees
shed their leaves it was certainly winter. On the way he crossed
wide, fast-flowing rivers, pushed through dense green forests and
saw wild animals of a kind he had never seen before.

All the same, he never met a living soul.

A year passed and Kuul Kihi shot an arrow into the setting

sun; another year went by and he sent a second arrow in the same direction. Yet in all that time he encountered not a single person.

A third year passed and Kuul Kihi loosed his last arrow; then half a year more was gone and, finally, only one day remained before the year was up.

He had now come to the bank of a broad river and, being footsore and weary, he sat down on a large stone to rest. Suddenly he was roused by the sound of voices muffled and faint. So great was his joy that he jumped to his feet and ran along the bank towards the sounds, hailing and shouting to the unknown persons. It was not long before he spotted a tall house standing on a high knoll above the bank. There were children playing nearby and sitting on a bench, watching them fondly, was a richly dressed man, a few years older than Kuul Kihi, seemingly lost in thought.

Kuul Kihi felt somehow shy in the presence of these strangers, for he had not looked upon his own kind for some years; but he plucked up courage and approached the house. When he stood before the man, he said:

'Nearly four years have passed since I left my home; all that time I have been walking toward the rising sun without ever hearing the sound of a human voice, and I am overjoyed to have found you. Pray tell me what are your thoughts, for I fear I have intruded upon them.'

The master of the house spoke up:

'I was thinking of my dear brother whom I lost some thirty years ago. I was a boy then and he but a child; and once we went with our father into the forest. I was to look after my brother and see he came to no harm. But I was so busy watching a squirrel in the trees that I did not notice my brother wandering off into the forest. That was how I came to lose him.

'I've never been able to find him since, search as I have; and I've never forgiven myself for having been so careless. On his death-bed my father told me I was not to despair, for even should fifty years pass, I would have my brother back again one day and we would live together as before. He left the two of us a thousand horses, this handsome house and many costly things. But I alone have the use of them, since my dear brother is not here to share them with me.

'But tell me, stranger, who are you? Whence come you and what is your name?'

Kuul Kihi told the man his name and how for nearly twenty years he had lived with his wife on a hilltop far away, hunted and fished for a living and finally gone off to seek his kinsfolk.

'If my wife does not hear from me by tomorrow,' he said, 'she will think me dead and she will leave our home for ever.'

Now the older man had always cherished the hope of finding his brother and now wondered whether this stranger might be he. He said nothing of this to the wayfarer, but he knew that his brother had a large birthmark on the sole of his left foot. So he and his wife gave Kuul Kihi food and drink and put him to bed, waiting for him to fall asleep before looking at his foot.

As soon as the newcomer was fast asleep, the host crept quietly to his bedside and drew back the blanket. At once he let out a gasp of surprise, for there on the sole of the sleeping man's left foot was a large brown birthmark.

'My brother! I have found my long-lost brother at last!' he cried. 'Come, everyone, and see, it is my dear brother.'

And he threw his arms round the sleeping man.

Kuul Kihi awoke with a start and was amazed to find himself in his host's embrace. When he learned that this rich and kindly man was his own brother he could scarcely believe his good luck; yet there was the birthmark to show it was indeed so. Though he racked his brain for evidence, he could think of nothing save that he had been brought up by an old woman who called herself his mother – though she had told him once that his real mother had died. And when he came to manhood he married her only daughter.

'Wait,' he said. 'Let us not be too hasty to rejoice before we have proved that we are really brothers. If anyone knows my past it can only be my wife, for her mother, who is now dead, may have told her something of it. I must hasten back to her lest she think me lost for ever.'

With this the older man had to agree.

Next morning he brought a fast horse for Kuul Kihi, saying:

'Ride home and bring your wife here, for I would like to hear the story from her lips. Make haste now, as I do not like to be parted from you now that I have found you at last. I already think of you as my brother, younger son of the bold warrior Ersyo.'

Kuul Kihi mounted the horse, gave a loud shout and, with the wind whistling in his ears, galloped across the plain towards the setting sun. Some time passed before he saw in the distance his own house standing atop the familiar hill. At the sight of it his heart began to pound, fearful lest his dear wife should have already left.

He arrived just in time: she was just about to depart. How glad and relieved she was to see her husband safe and sound. The very next day they rode to the house of Ersyo the warrior's elder son.

It was not until they arrived at the house that Kuul Kihi asked his wife if her mother had told her anything of the past, of how he had come to be living in their house.

'All she said was that she found you wandering in the forest, almost dead from fear and hunger,' his wife said. 'You were only a little boy then and she took you in and brought you up as her son. There was nothing to tell who you were except for a bow and arrow you had with you. These she put away and made me promise never to part with them. They are here in my bag.'

She reached into her bag and brought out a small, skilfully contrived bow and an arrow specially made for it.

'Why, this bow and arrow were fashioned by my own father's hands,' cried the elder brother at the sight of them. 'There, that is all the proof that is needed. Now we know beyond doubt that you are indeed my brother.'

The two brothers embraced and wept tears of happiness. The elder brother divided between them all that their father had left, and after that invited guests from all parts of the land to a great celebration.

Together the two brothers defended the Dolgan people against their enemies and proved worthy of their father, the mighty warrior Ersyo. Throughout their lives the Dolgans lived in peace and tranquillity. Even today, whenever the Dolgan folk hear of any war on earth, they shake their heads and say:

'What a pity the mighty warrior Ersyo and his two sons are no more, for had they been alive this would not have been.'

THE ONE-EYED MAN AND THE
WOMAN-VIXEN

There once lived a one-eyed man who spent each night at home with his wife, but left her each day at dawn and went off alone. His wife never knew why her husband did not come home by day, where he passed his time or what he did. And she dearly wished to know.

So one day, when he had left home early, she followed him and came to the place where he spent his days. Yet when she drew close she saw that he had changed his form: now even his one eye was gone and he was more ugly than ever. So disgusted was she that she made up her mind to leave him for good.

The very next day she set out to seek her fortune and on the way she met a giant. That giant snatched her up and slung her over his shoulder, carrying her off to the top of a high mountain. Once there he flung her through the opening of a great yurta. And there, sore and scared, she began to weep. Her clothes were all torn and she suffered terribly from the cold, now bitterly regretting that she had deserted her husband because she thought him ugly. And when she thought of that, she cried all the more until suddenly she heard a voice:

'Come on, dry your tears. Look up and you'll see the skins of land birds hanging above you. Take them and put them on.'

The woman looked up and noticed a grass-braided basket hanging on the wall; in it she found a jacket made of crow skins. Taking the jacket she went to put it on but no matter how hard she tried, she could not: it was too small. Once more she burst into tears, and again she heard the voice whispering to her:

'Come now, do not cry. Look up and you will find the skins of

174

land animals; take them and put them on.'

Looking up she found some fox skins; she took them down and tried to put them on. This time they fitted her well and soon she felt quite warm. Dressed in her new fox coat she began to seek a way out of the yurta; eventually she found it and set off on her journey home.

On the way, she felt thirsty and stopped at a stream to drink; but when she caught a reflection of herself in the clear water she was horrified to see that she had grown long fox's ears.

On she went and it was not long before she felt someone was behind her; as she turned her head she saw that it was her own fox's tail trailing behind her. Although she tried to shake free of the large red brush, she was unable to do so and had to proceed with the tail.

Shortly she arrived at the seashore where her father was just setting out to hunt seals. He was paddling along in his canoe when he saw the vixen standing on the shore not seeming to fear him at all. Yet when he came up the beach and tried to seize her, she evaded his grasp and kept out of reach. He threw her some seal meat which she devoured greedily before running off into the trees. Only when darkness had fallen did she steal into her father's settlement toward his yurta; many times she tried to enter his home, but each time she moved her head to pass inside, the head itself seemed to jerk to the side. And she was unable to pass.

In the end she made her way sadly to the fields and, there, folk say, she remains to this day.

MISTRESS OF FIRE

This story began a long time ago when all Selkups lived in four great tents on a single camping ground.

One day the men went to the forest to hunt, leaving the women and children behind in the tents. At the end of three days, the hunters had still not returned and one of the women came out of her yurta to chop some firewood. She brought logs into the tent, threw them on to the hearth and, lighting a fire, drew close to it with her baby at her breast. Soon the fire was crackling merrily while the mother warmed her baby by its glow.

All of a sudden, a spark flew up, fell on the child and burnt him. In his pain the baby screamed and the mother sprang up very angry with the fire.

'Ungrateful fire!' she cried. 'I give you logs to burn and you harm my child. You'll get no more from me. I'll chop you up instead, pour water on you and put you out.'

Leaving her baby in the cot and taking up an axe, she first chopped away at the flames and then, picking up a potful of water, she dashed it on to the burning embers.

'Just you try to burn anyone now!' she cried. 'I've put you out good and proper; not a spark's left.'

So it was: the fire burned no more. It was dark now in the tent and so cold that the baby began to wail even louder than before. The mother became frightened by what she had done and tried to light the fire again; and although she tried hard, she blew and puffed, all her efforts were in vain.

As the baby's cries continued, she ran to her neighbors for a light. But the moment she pulled back the tent flap, the fire on her neighbor's hearth went out and could not be rekindled. The same happened at every tent, even though she would open the

tent flap just a fraction: the moment she appeared, the fires
would splutter and smoke and then go out altogether.

All her kinsfolk scolded her and one old woman told her she
had plainly offended the Mistress of Fire.

The mother began to cry at her plight: there was now no fire
anywhere in the camp, no one could light one, and it was dark
and cold in the tents.

'Come, let us go to your tent, girl,' the old woman said. 'I wish
to see what you have done to anger the Mistress.'

Back in her own tent, the baby was crying even more than ever
and it was colder than anywhere else in the camp. The old
woman took two sticks of wood and rubbed them together in an
effort to start a fire; yet though she worked patiently to kindle
some fire, nothing came of it. But then, to her surprise, she saw a
faint light appear on the hearth; she bent lower and peered hard.
At first she could scarcely see anything, it being so dark; then
gradually she made out the figure of an old crone crouching
there. As the woman stared, the old crone's lined and withered
face grew bright and rosy, seeming to radiate a glow as from a
fire.

And then she spoke:

'Do not try to light a fire for you will not succeed. The mistress
of this tent has offended me gravely, and I cannot forgive her.
She chopped at my head and threw water in my face.'

'I knew that silly girl had done something wicked,' said the old
woman. 'Please do not be angry with us all, Fire Mistress, she is
young and stupid and has caused us all to suffer. Give us fire, I
beg of you.'

The Fire Mistress was silent, unmoved by the woman's pleas.
After a long pause she finally spoke again:

'All right, I shall grant you fire on one condition: that stupid
girl must give me her son. From his heart I shall kindle a flame.
Knowing this, she will always respect fire and never treat it
thoughtlessly again.'

Turning to the young mother, the old woman said:

'Because of you all seven tribes of man remain without fire.
How are they to survive? There is nothing for it: though the

judgement be harsh, you must give up your son to save us all!'

The mother wept, remorseful at her thoughtless act and heart-broken at the judgement it had brought upon her. But there was nothing for it: if the tribes of man were to be saved she had to sacrifice her child. And so she did.

When she had given up her child, the Mistress herself towered over her like a huge flame and spoke thus:

'Know now, O Selkups, that you must never touch fire with any tool of iron unless you are in great need. And then you should seek my permission first. Mind my words well.'

With that she touched the logs with her fingertips, setting them alight. The flames immediately leapt up and spiralled up to the very roof of the sky as the Fire Mistress swept up the child and vanished with him into the flames. Neither were ever seen again.

'A legend will be born this day,' said the old woman to the grieving mother. 'From mouth to mouth the story will be told of how a fire was lit from the heart of your child. And it was done to save the Selkup tribes.'

THE TWO SUNS

Adyga the bold hunter lived in a tent beside the Amur River with his wife.

In those far-off times there were two suns in the sky. And those two suns pressed down upon the land, withered the trees and parched the grass; streams ran dry and even the mighty Amur gurgled its complaint against its stones; animals departed to more humid climes and birds flew off to seek the shade, for every creature found it hard to breathe in the torrid taiga.

Children were born to Adyga's wife, but did not live long upon the cruel earth. Poor Adyga grew very angry with the heartless suns and fashioned himself a bow of hardest wood.

The two suns never rose high in the sky, they would hang sullenly upon the crest of a distant hill.

One day, as the sun brothers mounted the hill and stood defiantly above it, Adyga drew back his bow, saying:

'Fly my arrow straight and true; pierce the sun's unyielding heart. You are our only hope.'

With a shrill whistle, the arrow sped straight to its mark and vanished into the burning soul of one of the suns. A great rumbling was to be heard as if the earth were turning over; and the wounded sun turned a deathly pale.

It formed the moon.

At once the other sun rose even higher in the sky, fearful of Adyga's arrows.

From that time a single Moon and Sun can be seen in the heavens. The trees soon began to grow again, the animals joyfully returned, the birds flew back to their nests, and children laughed along the banks of the Amur, as merrily as they do today.

WIFE FOR A WALRUS, LORD OF THE SEA

There was once an old man and his wife who were very poor. Many's the time they never knew the smell of good food, and many's the time they had to make do with the putrid fish cast up on the shore.

Now the old pair had a daughter who grew up to be very beautiful. And the young girl lived with her parents, hungered with them and, like them, ate whatever the sea might yield.

Late one winter the family remained without a scrap of food and did not know what to do. Every day the old man went down to the shore in the hope of finding dead fish or a rotting carcass of a seal, but though he wandered far along the beach he found nothing. Finally, he sat down upon a large rock, his head in his hands.

'How can I go home empty-handed?' he sighed. 'What will I feed my wife and daughter on?'

He sat there sorrowing for a long time, and when at twilight he had to leave, he cast a last hopeful glance at the sea; it had suddenly turned dark and menacing, then began to seethe and boil like water in a cauldron.

In awe he watched from behind the rock as the waves flung a huge whale upon the shore and at once six great walruses, lords of the sea, leapt out in pursuit, cut the whale to pieces with their sabers and then vanished back into the sea.

The old man hardly dared breathe; but, now all was still, he crept fearfully up to the dead whale and there, beside him, found a saber left by the walruses.

'The sea has brought me a rich present,' he cried, overjoyed.

Picking up the saber, he cut a good slice of meat from the whale and went home; he handed the meat and the saber to his wife who immediately hid the saber in a large chest, then stoked up the fire to cook the meat and feed her family.

Having eaten their fill, the old man and woman lay down to sleep. They slept soundly and it was past dawn by the time they awoke. Glancing round, they saw at once that all was not as it should be: their daughter was missing.

'Where has our child gone?' they cried in alarm. And as soon as the sun was up they set about searching for the girl. They looked high and low throughout the day until it was quite dark, but to no avail. When they came back to their choom, however, there was their daughter sitting at the entrance looking up at them sadly.

'Where have you been, my child?' the old woman asked.

But the daughter uttered not a sound, only wrung her hands.

The three of them went inside, yet none could sleep or talk. As they sat in silence, the daughter abruptly rose and made to leave the choom; no sooner did she step through the opening than she vanished into the air.

Spring followed winter in due course without her having returned and one day, while on the shore looking for fish, the old man found himself by the rock on which he had sat the previous year.

Now he sat on it again and gazed out to sea, thinking all the while of his dear daughter and wishing with all his heart that he could see her once more.

'Come to me, my child,' he whispered. 'Come to your old father, wherever you are, even from the depths of the sea.'

And as he gazed into the waters, he saw that the sea had turned dark and menacing; it seethed and boiled like water in a cauldron. Then six giant walruses, lords of the sea, rose from the depths on the crest of a wave and there, sitting on the back of the biggest, was his daughter.

A great trembling seized the old man, he began to weep and cry, saying over and over again:

'Oh, my child, my only child! You have come to me from the

181

bottom of the sea. Will you not speak one word to your father?'

'I will, Father, I will!' the daughter replied. 'Listen carefully to what I have to say: you angered the lords of the sea by taking their saber and I am made to pay for it. Go home and tell my mother of the punishment and return to this rock in a year.'

With that she vanished back into the sea, and the old man went home to tell his wife the news.

A year passed, spring came once more and the old man hurried down to the shore; sitting on the self-same rock, he fixed his gaze upon the sea.

'Come to me, my child,' he called softly. 'Come to me, wherever you are, even from the bottom of the sea.'

All at once, a huge wave struck the shore, and out of the depths came a giant walrus, the Lord of the Sea himself, with the old man's beautiful daughter on his back. She stepped gently down and stood before her father. The old man looked and could hardly credit what his eyes saw.

For there stood his daughter, more radiant than ever, her dark hair almost to her waist; and in her arms lay a smiling baby.

The young mother was holding the baby for her father to see.

'Come here no more, Father,' she told him, 'for I shall not be here for you to see. I am the wife of the Lord of the Sea and have borne him this son. From this day on I must remain with him at the bottom of the sea. Tell my mother that I am content and that she must not grieve or search for me. Henceforth neither of you shall want for anything: should you desire meat, come to the shore and you shall find it. I shall send as many seals as you wish. You may eat your fill and no longer want for food.'

With that she climbed on the walrus's back and he plunged back into the depths; he and the girl with her baby disappeared.

The old man turned for home to tell his wife of their daughter's fate.

'She will never come back to us,' he said. 'She has wed the Lord of the Sea and borne him a son; now she must remain at the bottom of the sea forever. She would have you know that she is content and you must not grieve for her. And one thing more: from now on we shall want for nothing.'

As the daughter had promised, so it was. The old man and woman lived on for a good many years. And whenever the old man came to the shore, he found seals there fresh from the sea; thus he and his wife came to know the taste of good food for the rest of their lives.

Yet never again did they see their dear daughter.

TYNAGIRGIN AND GITGILIN

A young Chukchi lived alone with his grandmother. One day he said to her:

'I mean to go to Tynagirgin the Giant and seek a wife.'

'As you will,' answered the old woman.

Now Tynagirgin and Gitgilin were brothers to one wife and lived far out in the tundra; they were feared by all the Chukchi because they were evil spirits as well as fearsome giants.

But the young man was not afraid because he was a shaman.

When he arrived at the great yaranga of the two giants, he entered before they could even bid him 'etti' – welcome! He stood before them on the hearth and announced his mission.

Tynagirgin turned angrily to his brother:

'Let us teach this young intruder a lesson!'

So the giants brought the young man to the centre of the yaranga, pushed their iron cooking pot aside and said:

'Take a look through this hole at the life below.'

As the lad stared down into the underworld he was able to make out several large settlements with crowds of people in them. Some were fishing, some hunting polar bear, and yet others curing seal and walrus hides.

As they closed the opening, the giants said:

'That is not all, now we shall show you something even more interesting. Come and see.'

The three of them went out into the snow and, all of a sudden, a great roaring was heard; as they made their way towards the sound, the earth heaved and yawned and the two giants crowded round the hole in the ground.

'Ah! Ooh! Oi-yoi-yoi! How exciting, how interesting it is down there!' they exclaimed. 'Now it is your turn, lad, just look below.'

The young man came forward and bent down to take a look.
As he did so, the two giants pushed him through the hole and he
plunged down towards a great boiling, hissing iron pot. While in
flight, however, he quickly turned himself into a mosquito and
flew up in the nick of time.

Leaving him to his fate, the two giant brothers returned to
their yaranga. In the meantime, the boy had spotted a tiny crack
in the ground, and he flew up into the outside world again and
followed the two giants.

In the yaranga meanwhile, Tynagirgin and Gitgilin were roaring with laughter at the trick they had played on the stupid boy.

'Boiled guts is all that is left of our bold wife-seeker now,' they
chuckled.

As they stood there congratulating themselves, the very same
young man coughed loudly behind them, startling the two giants.

'Is it really you, wife-seeker?' they asked.

'It is I, the very same,' he answered coolly.

'Then you must accompany us to the cliffs; it is even more
exciting there,' they said.

All three made their way to the cliffs that towered above the
mighty ocean. Coming to the very edge, first the two giants
looked below, exclaiming:

'Ah! Ooh! Oi-yoi-yoi! How exciting, how fascinating! Just
take a look at that.'

As the young lad bent forward to look the two giants gave him
such a shove that he fell headlong over the cliffs. However, as he
plunged down towards the rocks below he swiftly turned himself
into a sparrow-hawk, spread his wings wide and alighted gently
upon a sea-spattered rock. Glancing about him he saw human
blood staining the rocks around and dried innards strung over
the outcrops; these were from all the people the two evil giants
had pushed over the cliffs.

The hawk soared upwards and flew after Tynagirgin and
Gitgilin as they made their way home. Entering their yaranga,
the two giants began to chortle at their deed.

'Smashed to grains of salt, our wife-hunter,' they roared. 'He's
probably hanging his guts out to dry on the rocks right now!'

In fact, at that very moment, the young man coughed loudly at the entrance to the tent.

'Oh no! He's back again', the giants stuttered in amazement. 'We shall have to out-shamanize him.'

So the giants put out all the lamps and called the visitor to the center of the hearth.

And Tynagirgin began to shamanize: he beat his drum in the darkness, called up the evil spirit Kochatko, the Polar Bear, and ordered him to deal with the intruder.

But as soon as the evil spirit had appeared, the young man turned himself into a mountain goat and climbed sure-footedly high into the topmost rafters of the tent. The beating of the drum continued for some time penetrating all corners of the tent until, finally, the shaman drove out all the spirits and declared triumphantly:

'Light the fire. Our wife-seeker is surely nothing but a withered bladder by now.'

However, the young man climbed down from the rafters and sat quietly with his back to the wall.

When the fire was rekindled, its light fell upon him sitting there calmly smoking a pipe. Astonished, the two giants handed him their drum and bade him display his shaman powers.

Yet the lad declined their drum.

'I have my own,' he said.

Taking a tiny tambourine from round his neck, he began to tap it softly from the center outward; and as he tapped it, the tambourine grew bigger and bigger until it was almost as big as the lad himself. And when it was large enough, he began his singing and whirling, calling up the Spirit of the Sea Breeze. Then, the sea, rushing into the yaranga with a roar, crashed its great ice floes against the tent walls and put out the fire. Terrified, the two giant brothers fled.

Then the young shaman took a deep breath, swallowed the pretty wife and headed for home. Once there he breathed out the wife and began to live with her himself. In no time at all she bore him two handsome sons.

All went well until one day his grandmother cried out in alarm:

'Oh dear, two terrible giants are coming this way; they are doubtless seeking their wife. Give them back their woman, my son, and let us live in peace.'

'No, they shan't have her back,' shouted the lad. He swiftly made a woman out of snow and daubed signs upon the faces of the two women in his tent to protect them from the evil spirits.

Just then, Tynagirgin and Gitgilin came into the yaranga looking for their woman, who was busy with her children.

'I was wrong to take your woman,' said the young man to the two visitors. 'I feel sorry for you; you must be very lonely. But the woman has a sister. Call her in will you, Grannie?'

The poor grandmother did not know whom to call. As she hesitated, a voice came from outside the tent, calling:

'Leen, leen, leen!'

It was the snowwoman coming.

Round the tent flap appeared a woman's head, an exceedingly lovely pale figure. The two giants immediately took her off to their home.

Once back in their yaranga, they placed her between them on their reindeer-skin bed and went to sleep contented. However, in the middle of the night, they woke up shivering and found their new wife gone.

The snowwoman had melted clean away.

So Tynagirgin and Gitgilin remained without a woman. Meanwhile, the young man's wife bore him many children and they all lived well.

That's how it was.

There, I have killed the storm!

NIRAIDAK

Long, long ago when the earth had just been born and the blue sky was being woven above, there stood a small island at a junction where the longest rivers met. And on that island was a tent fashioned from eight branches of rose willow and three squirrel skins. In the tent lived a man named Niraidak who was so small that he wore a coat of two sable skins, a hat of a mole skin and mittens each of a whole mouse skin.

Niraidak also had a knife of deer bone and a small, hornless deer on whose back he rode as on a horse. Aside from his deer he had no one, neither mother nor father, sister nor brother. He was quite alone in the world and passed his days hunting wild animals and catching fish. A squirrel to him was as big as a fox to an ordinary man, a doe as big as a moose, and the tiniest bird as big as an eagle. And when he killed any one of them he felt very pleased with himself, for his needs were as small as his frame.

Time went on and since there was no one he could compare himself to, he began to think he was the biggest person in the world.

One day, Niraidak made up his mind to do three things: to see how other folk lived, to measure his strength against that of a giant, and to find himself a wife besides. As to the last, he decided he would wed the most beautiful woman in the world.

So he summoned his hornless deer and whispered in his ear:

'Come, my only friend, turn into a fire-breathing boar, fly high above the trees and bear me to a land where the strongest of giants and the most beautiful of women dwell.'

In no time at all, the deer became a fire-breathing boar; Niraidak sat on his back and away they soared over the forest. Presently they reached a great chasm on whose opposite side stood the giant Dioloni – Man of Stone.

They flew across the chasm, and Niraidak dismounted so as to creep up on the giant; he was quite close when he unexpectedly tripped over a twig and fell, hitting his nose against Dioloni's big toe.

The giant stirred.

'Who is that tickling my toes?' he said, and seeing the tiny figure by his feet he pick him up and placed him gently on his palm.

'I am the great Niraidak', the little man squeaked. 'I have no fear of you, Dioloni the Giant. Beware, for I am going to slay you.'

Flourishing his deer-bone knife he jumped up and down on the giant's hand, screaming at the top of his voice and looking very fierce, thinking to scare the giant.

Dioloni roared with laughter and, so as not to harm the funny little man, picked him up gently between two fingers and put him inside his shirt. At first Niraidak was taken aback by this, but he then crept down to the giant's sleeve, crawled along the long tunnel into his trousers, slid down his trouser leg and sprang to the ground. In a few strides he reached his faithful mount, leapt on his back and was off like the wind. Only when they had rounded a hill did he turn back to shout and wave his fist:

'Take care, Dioloni the Giant, next time I'll skin you and crush your bones to dust!'

On they rode until they reached a camp where the most beautiful women in the world lived. And here the little man had all the women lined up for his inspection and, after gazing at each of them admiringly, he selected the one he judged the prettiest of all, placed her down in front of him on the boar's back and set off for home. They arrived soon enough and Niraidik unsaddled his fire-breathing boar.

He was about to lead his new wife into his tent when he saw that it would not do: after all, his tent was made only of eight branches of rose willow and three squirrel skins. It was much too small for his wife. So he set to building a new tent and when it was ready, he stood back to admire his handiwork. He thought it was magnificent, as big and spacious as the heavens!

Leaving his wife in the new home, Niraidak went down to the river to fish. Very soon he had caught as many as twenty-five fishes; he stuck them all on a stick, but when he tried to lift it he found it was much too heavy for him. There was nothing for it but to return to fetch his wife.

'I've caught so many big fish, wife,' he said, 'that I can't carry them all home by myself. You'll have to give me a hand.'

The wife was delighted and fairly flew down to the river.

'Where are all the big fish?' she gasped in surprise.

'Do you not see them?' Niraidak said. 'There is the river, there is the bank and here are the fish!'

The wife looked down at the tiny fishes stuck on a stick and stamped her foot crossly. She picked up the stick with one hand, carried it back to the tent and cooked the fish; and though she consumed them all, she was as hungry as ever. She screamed at her husband, told him how useless he was to her and packed him off to fetch more food. Niraidak told her to lie down, placed a stone on her belly that she might not feel hungry and went off to the forest.

When he had gone, the woman said to herself:

'What use is this little shrimp of a husband to me? I'll starve to death and have no clothing on my back if I remain here with him.'

And off she went to a village where there lived strong and considerate men who did not refuse their wives anything they asked.

As for Niraidak, he still lives all by himself in his solitary tent and to this day is without a wife. And yet, can you believe it, he is happy and carefree and no longer regrets his solitude.

MAN-BEAR

One time many Yukagirs fell ill and there was little their shamans could do to help. More and more people died.

So one young man decided to seek help. He traveled downstream along the River Kolyma, though found no sign of any camp. Eventually, he came to the mouth of the river, gazed far into the distance, but saw nothing save an ocean of water in front of him. There was nothing for it but to return home.

However, winter had set in and it was very cold. The young Yukagir was much afraid, certain he would freeze to death in the taiga; and he began to search for a cave where he might shelter. As he approached some foothills of a snow-covered mountain, he suddenly saw a ragged hole halfway up the slope.

'A bear surely lives in that warm den,' he thought. 'But I'm bound to perish in the snow anyway; if the bear's asleep I might be able to slay it and eat it. And if it isn't, it will then eat me. Never mind, I shall have to take what comes.'

The Yukagir pulled aside the brush covering the hole and crawled in. It was warm and cosy inside, but he was at once met by a huge she-bear. Knocking him over with her muzzle, the bear replaced the brush across the entrance and then lay down alongside the man.

He was very frightened, but since the bear did not touch him further, his fear began to lessen. All the same, his belly cried out for food and, as if reading his thoughts, the bear brought him some dried fish and meat. He ate until he was quite full.

Thus the Yukagir passed the entire winter with the she-bear. Spring came. Each day the she-bear went hunting, bringing the man food for him to cook. And life went on as before.

In the summertime, the she-bear gave birth to a son who grew very fast and whose strength was most uncommon. By the end of summer, the man-bear was almost as tall as his father and he would often ask the Yukagir:

'Where do you come from? How do Yukagirs live? Let us go and see your people.'

And the Yukagir would answer:

'I myself would like to see my people, only I don't know the way.'

In the end, the man-bear said:

'Then let us go together; I shall discover where people live. My nose will lead me.'

So off they went: the Yukagir and the man-bear. They walked on through the days and nights until the entire summer had passed. And when they came to the place where people lived, the Yukagir's wife and son were overjoyed to see him. But everyone took fright at the man-bear; they did not like him at all. Only the Yukagir's young son was fond of him, and they would wrestle and play together. It was not long, however, before the man-bear tired of life among people in the camp and longed for the wide open spaces of the taiga. So, in a while, he left the Yukagirs and set off by himself across the plain.

After several days he came upon five hunters.

'Where are you bound?' the men asked. 'Since you travel alone you may care to join us?'

The man-bear gladly accepted their offer, and the six continued on their way until they came to a cottage in the middle of the forest. Since it was late, they decided to spend the night there. Next morning, the man-bear and four of the hunters went off to seek a breakfast, leaving the fifth hunter behind.

No sooner had the hunters disappeared into the trees than the master of the cottage returned: he was a little old man with a long white beard. So long was his beard that when he stood inside the cottage the end of his beard lay outside in the yard. And he was not at all pleased to have company.

'What are you doing here?' he screeched. 'Get out of my house at once!'

At the sight of the weird old man, the hunter burst out

laughing. Again the little old man screamed at him. It seemed to the hunter that he could pick the old man up with one hand and toss him out of the house. And when the little old man shrieked a third time, the hunter finally lost patience. He went to seize the old fellow but, all of a sudden, he found himself wrapped up in his white beard, jerked up by the feet and dragged across the floor. Then he felt his head being thrust through a hole in a wooden block – and he was stuck fast.

The poor man pulled and stretched this way and that, and finally succeeded in getting free. But he was so weary from his exertions that he lay down and immediately fell asleep, quite forgetting to prepare wood for the fire and water for the pot.

Towards evening, the man-bear and the four hunters returned to the cottage, and at once set about their sleeping companion for his laziness. He did not dare tell them how the little old man had got the better of him.

Next morning, again the man-bear and the hunters went hunting leaving another of their companions behind. Once more the little old man arrived and put the lone hunter's head in the wooden block.

Thus, in turn, each of the five hunters suffered the ire of the little master. And each of them was too ashamed to admit to the others that such a tiny man had defeated them.

At last it came to the turn of the man-bear to remain behind. When the five hunters had left, he lay down to sleep, but was soon woken up by the shrieks of the little old man who seized the man-bear and dragged him outside into the yard. But the man-bear was very strong: he seized the old fellow by his beard and tied him with it to the trunk of a tree.

When the hunters returned, they found the man-bear sitting outside the cottage looking pleased with himself. He told them all that had happened and he took them to the tree. Yet all that remained of the little old man was his long beard wound round the tree. The hunters all recognized the beard at once and confessed that the old fellow had defeated each of them. And they praised the man-bear.

They all set off now in pursuit of the little old man, following the white hairs strewn upon the ground, and they eventually arrived at a large rock in a clearing. First the hunters tried to shift the rock, but it was too heavy for them; then the man-bear stepped forward and thrust it aside with ease. The white hairs led down beneath the ground. First the hunters tried to climb along the tunnel but they soon got stuck and could go no farther. Then the man-bear crawled down and he had no trouble at all.

He climbed down and down until at last he found himself inside a yurta. And there was an old, old woman sitting and crying, because someone had torn off her husband's beard; his beard had been his strength, and without it he had died.

When the man-bear asked the old women to tell him the way back to the daylight, she thought to get her revenge.

'He is bound to lose his way and die underground,' she thought.

The man-bear set off from the yurta, walked straight ahead, then did everything the other way about: where the old woman told him to turn right, he turned left; where she said turn left, he took the right turning. At each turning, he came upon a rich yurta, entered, yet found it empty. Finally he came to the very last yurta: no path led on from there. As he listened outside, he could hear the lovely voice of a young woman singing. Raising the bear-skin flap at the entrance, he looked in and saw a beautiful girl sitting as if waiting for him.

Bowing low, be told her how her mother, the old, old wife of the little old man, had sent him to her with the invitation to be his wife. The girl was silent for a time and then at last gave her consent. Thereupon, she took him by the hand and led him through a secret tent flap into the self-same tunnel that he had first entered.

All this time the five hunters had been sitting by the tunnel entrance waiting for the man-bear to return. One argued that the man-bear must be dead, while another maintained that such a strong, brave man would survive. And then, suddenly, out of the tunnel appeared the head of the beautiful young girl. At once the hunters rushed at her, dragging her up above the ground and knocking the man-bear back down the tunnel and closing it with the large rock.

Once they had the girl among them, the hunters began to quarrel, each wanting to make her his wife. They fought and fought until all that remained were two hunters equal in strength. Since neither could conquer the other, they had to agree to share her as their wife.

Meanwhile, the man-bear turned back along the tunnel and wandered alone along the underground pathways. On and on he walked until he heard birdsong; turning towards the sound, he found himself before another yurta. Inside was a young girl even lovelier than the first. And by her side was a white eagle.

'I shall show you the way out', she said, 'if you promise to find a husband for me. I am tired of living here along. My eagle will carry you on his wings up to the daylight.'

The man-bear agreed.

'First I'll fly up above,' he said, 'and when I return I shall take you to your husband.'

At that the girl ordered the white eagle to take the man-bear on its wings. Hardly had be sat on the eagle's shoulders than all beneath him trembled and he flew up to the daylight. Dismounting from the eagle, he hurried to the cottage in the middle of the forest.

When the two hunters saw the man-bear coming they took fright. And as the man-bear came in, he seized one hunter with his right hand, the other with his left and, before they could move, he banged their heads together so hard, they burst asunder.

'Now you shall be my wife,' he said to the girl. 'But if ever you leave me for another, I shall treat you as I did those hunters. Just wait for me here while I go back underground.'

The girl laughed happily and the man-bear left the cottage with a light heart. As soon as the eagle saw him, it flew down from a tree and placed the man-bear upon its broad shoulders.

'Fly me to your mistress,' he told the white eagle.

Away flew the eagle and before the man-bear had time to look round, he was standing in the same yurta he had left shortly before. Going up to the girl, he said:

'I have returned to you, let us now go together to seek your husband.'

The girl sat astride the eagle behind the man-bear and they flew swiftly into the sunlight and on to the cottage in the forest. There they stopped to pick up the man-bear's wife and flew on to the distant camp of the Yukagirs.

The Yukagir was overjoyed to see his second son, the man-bear. His first son was now fully grown and even more delighted to see his brother; how surprised he was to find the man-bear had brought him a lovely wife.

But the man-bear did not stay long among the Yukagirs; he soon returned to the taiga and lived out his days there with his wife that he had brought up from the underground yurta.

Folk say that you may meet just such a man-bear in the Siberian forest even now; or if not him, then his grandson. You may even catch a glimpse of the old white eagle flying alone over the taiga. And the Yukagirs, they say, are all descended from bears.

DAUGHTER OF THE MOON, SON OF THE SUN

All through the day the Sun rides through the sky in his golden sledge. At dawn it is drawn by Polar Bear, at midday by Buck Reindeer, and at dusk by Doe Reindeer. Many are the chores the Sun must attend to: granting life to all that lives, nourishing the green moss and trees, giving light and strength to all beasts and birds and to the Saami people, that they may grow strong and multiply.

Towards twilight, when the Sun gets weary, he sinks down to the sea; all he then wishes is to rest and sleep, to regain his powers for the coming day.

But one evening, as Doe Reindeer drew the Sun towards his watery couch, the Sun's handsome son Peivalke spoke up.

'Father, it is time for me to marry.'

'Have you chosen a bride?' asked the Sun, wearily.

'Not yet. I have tried my golden boots on all the earthly maids and not one could wear them. Their feet are so heavy and clumsy, they cannot follow me up to the sky.'

'Then you have sought wrongly,' said the Sun, with a yawn. 'Tomorrow I shall speak to the Moon: she has a daughter. Though she is poorer than us, the Moon's daughter does dwell in the heavens and will make you a worthy bride.'

So the Sun rose early as day dawned, just as his neighbor the Moon was about to take her rest.

'Tell me, my pale companion', he said, 'is it not true that you have a daughter? I have found a worthy husband for her – she is indeed fortunate, for he is none other than my own son Peivalke.'

The Moon's bright countenance grew dim.

'My child is still too young. When I hold her close I hardly notice she is there; a puff of wind would bear her off. How can such a mite marry your son?'

'It matters not,' said the Sun. 'My tent is spacious and bountiful. She will be nourished well and will soon grow strong. Come, bring her to my son.'

'Oh no!' cried the Moon, aghast, and swiftly drew a white cloud about her child. 'Your Peivalke would scorch her delicate skin. What is more, she is already promised to Nainas, the Northern Lights. There he is now walking proudly across the ocean down below.'

'So that's it then!' said the Sun, gruffly. 'You reject my son for those miserable colored stripes? Lest you be unmindful, my humble companion, it is I who give life to all things. I am all-powerful.'

'Your power, neighbor, is but half the power there is,' murmured the Moon, softly. 'When dusk comes your powers recede into the night. And throughout the dark night? And the long winter? Where is your power then? Nainas shines on in winter too, piercing the gloom of night with his cheerful rays.'

These words only angered the Sun even more.

'I'll wed my son to your daughter, just see if I don't!' he blazed.

Thunder rolled across the heavens, the wind howled, the waves towered white with rage about the ocean, and the mountains shook in dread. The herds of reindeer huddled close and the Saami tribes trembled in corners of their summer shelters.

The Moon scurried away into the darkness of the night.

'I must keep my child safe from the Sun's angry gaze,' she thought.

Looking down from the sky she spied a small island in the middle of a lake where an old man and his wife lived.

'To that old pair,' the Moon said, 'I shall entrust my daughter. She will be safe there.'

By and by the Sun tired of his ranting: the thunder became still, the wind's wail died, and the waves settled back into the sea. And it was just about that time that the old man and his wife went into the forest to strip birch bark for sandals. They were astonished to hear a tiny voice crying above their heads:

'Niekia, Nickia, help me, help me.'

And there on a branch of a fir tree they saw a silver cradle rocking to and fro. As the old man reached to take it down, he saw a child lying there; she was like any other save that she gleamed as moonlight, a silver pallor covering her tender skin.

The old pair carried the cradle home, overjoyed at their good fortune. They tended her carefully, brought her up as their own daughter, and she did all they told her dutifully. Yet every night, before she went to bed, she would leave the hut, raise her pallid face to the Moon, lift up her arms and shine more brightly than before. When in playful mood she would call 'Niekia, Niekia' and melt away to nothing, leaving but the merry echo of her laughter.

So the old folk called her Niekia.

As the days passed, Niekia grew into a tall and slender maid with a bright face as round as cloudberries, her fair braids strung like silver threads. The lovely moon-maiden learned to make quilts of reindeer hide and embroider them with beads and silver. In the passage of time, word reached the Sun that on the island in that lake there lived a maid uncommon to the daughters of men. So he sent his son Peivalke to seek her out; and no sooner did the radiant young Sun gaze upon the silver maid than he fell deeply in love with her.

'Earth maiden, try on these golden boots,' said Peivalke.

Niekia blushed, but did as she was bid. Straightaway, she cried out in pain:

'Oh, they are burning my feet! How hot they are.'

'You will get used to them,' smiled Peivalke, reassuringly.

But before his eyes she melted into a misty haze and the golden boots stood empty on the ground.

Wrapped in quivering moonbeams, Niekia hid in the forest until nightfall. Then, as the Moon rose in the sky, Niekia followed her mother's light through the forest and across the cold tundra. At last, as dawn was breaking, she came to the shores of the ocean, to a lonely hut standing on its barren strand. Without a thought, Niekia entered the hut and found it empty. It was so untidy that she at once fetched a pail of sea-water and set to washing the hut. Her work done, she turned herself into an old spindle, hung herself up on the wall, and fell asleep.

As twilight cast its dark shadows upon the shore, heavy footsteps woke Niekia and she saw a group of warrios enter, all clad in silver armor, and each more handsome and stronger than the next. They were the Northern Lights led by their eldest brother, Nainas.

'Our hut is so clean,' said Nainas in amazement. 'A good housewife has visited us. Though I know not where she is hiding, I can feel the keen gaze of her eyes upon us.'

The brothers sat down to supper and when they had finished they began a mock battle among themselves, striking at one another with their sabers, making white sparks and crimson flashes that danced and soared into the sky. Then, tired from their sword-fight, the brothers sang songs about the bold warriors of the sky, each flying off in turn until at last only Nainas remained.

'Now, dear housewife,' he pleaded, 'please show yourself. Should you be of respected years, you shall be a mother to us. Should you be of middle years, you shall be our sister; and should you be yet young, you shall be my bride.'

'Here I am, judge for yourself,' said a soft voice behind him.

As he turned he saw a slim and lovely figure standing in the dim light of early dawn. And he recognized the lovely daughter of the Moon.

'Will you be my wife, Niekia?' he asked.

'Yes, Nainas,' she answered, so quietly he could barely hear her.

Just at that moment the first flush of dawn spread across the sky as the top of the Sun's head appeared.

'Wait for me here, Niekia,' cried Nainas, and was gone.

Every evening, Nainas and his brothers flew back to their home on the shore, fought their sword battle and then, at sunrise, flew away again.

'Please stay with me for just one day,' Niekia begged Nainas.

'That I cannot,' said Nainas. 'Across the ocean I must engage in the battle of the skies. Should I remain, the Sun would pierce me right through with his shafts of fire.'

As she waited in her lonely hut, Niekia wondered how she might detain her dear Nainas. And in her solitude she sang a song to her beloved:

> *'He is tall like a mountain ash,*
> *His hair covers his shoulders*
> *Like squirrels' tails.*
> *When he disappears*
> *I lie down in my hut.*
> *Oh, how long is a spring day?*
> *But the evening comes*
> *And through a hole in the hut*
> *I see my love coming.*
> *When he enters and looks at me*
> *My heart melts*
> *Like snow in the sun.'*

When she had finished, an idea came to her: she would make a quilt of reindeer hide, and embroider on it the stars and the Milky Way. That she did and, before the brothers returned home, she hung the quilt beneath the ceiling of the hut.

When night fell, Nainas flew home with his brother warriors. They played their games, had their supper, sang songs and lay down to rest. Nainas slept soundly. As dawn approached his eyes opened several times but, seeing the starlit sky with the Milky Way above him, he imagined it to be still night, too early to rise.

Niekia crept outside quietly some time after day had dawned, but forgot to close the hut door: in an instant, Nainas opened his eyes and saw the bright light of morning shining through the open door; he saw the Polar Bear pulling the Sun's golden sledge through the sky. At once he dashed from the hut calling his brothers after him.

But it was too late.

The Sun saw him, and sent down a shaft of fire that pinned him to the ground. Poor Niekia realized too late what she had done: she ran to her Nainas, shielding him from the Sun with her own body.

As she did so, Nainas struggled to his feet and flew off to safety in the heavens. The Sun seized Niekia by her braid, burned her with his fiery gaze and summoned his son Peivalke.

'You may burn me to a cinder, but I shall never marry Peivalke,' wept the daughter of the Moon.

In his fury, the Sun flung Niekia into the arms of her mother. And Mother Moon caught her, pressed her to her breast and still holds her safe and close to this day.

If you look closely at the moon, you will see the shadow of Niekia's fair face upon her mother's bosom. Niekia is there, watching the pale glimmer over the ocean of the battle of the Northern Lights across the evening sky, and pining for her beloved Nainas.

GLOSSARY

abaasy: Yakut evil spirit which appears only at night, being unable to bear the daylight

Akanidi: daughter of the Sun in many Saami (Lapp) tales

bakari: a shaman's long fur boots (Nivkh)

caribou: deer of northern lands related to the reindeer

chan: an urn made of reindeer hide or carved wood

choom: a cone-shaped tent used by tundra nomads and made of reindeer skins placed on a frame of 30–40 sticks or bones; it usually measures 4–6 yards in diameter across an earthen floor

Coot: folk name used by Itelmen and other tribes for the raven; often a stupid and lascivious character

echuulgin: a hide chamber pot of the Chukchi; it has its own spirits and world

Ememcoot: son of Coot

ermine: animal about 18 inches long. In summer its fur is reddish-brown except for a white belly. In winter its fur turns white except for the black tip of its tail

homus: Yakut folk instrument rather like a Jew's harp: about 5 inches long consisting of a metal frame holding a thin metal strip. The frame is held in the mouth, which serves as a sound-box, the metal strip is twanged with the forefinger, and the pitch of the note is varied by altering the shape of the cavity of the mouth

igloo: Eskimo dwelling in the shape of a dome built of blocks of frozen snow

kayak: Eskimo canoe made of sealskins stretched taut over a light wooden frame, completely closed in about the paddler

kelet: evil spirit of the Chukchi

kangakei: similar to homus, but slightly bigger, used by Nivkhs

lynx: wildcat somewhat larger than the domestic cat, with long, tufted ears and a short tail

Milky Way: a spiral galaxy of which the solar system is a part, containing billions of stars; it is thought by many northern people to be a pebbly river with many islands

Mitti: wife of Coot

Northern Lights: aurora borealis: a colored glow visible at night in parts of Siberia; it has the appearance of a fan of ascending luminous streamers near the northern horizon. It is thought by some to be a special world inhabited by dead souls dancing around fires in the heavens

Oadz: old marsh witch in Saami tales

Olonho: Yakut epic poem, based on the wanderings of a mythical hero

olonhosut: folk bard and performer of the *Olonho*

Peivalke: son of the Sun in Saami tales

sable: small mammal related to the weasel and a native of Arctic regions; it is highly valued for its lustrous dark-brown fur

shaman: Siberian medicine-man

steppe: vast, treeless, level plain

taiga: coniferous forests separating the steppe and tundra

tundra: flat, treeless plain covered with mosses and lichens with a permanently frozen subsoil

tungak: Eskimo evil spirit who brings misfortunes like hunger, sickness and death

wolverine: mammal about 1 yard long, with thick blackish fur and pale forehead. Also known as glutton

yaranga: as choom, but used more by maritime natives and usually constructed out of walrus hides

yurta: a low mud or clay hut principally used by the Yakuts.

MAJOR WORKS OF REFERENCE

T. Armstrong, *Russian Settlement in the North*, London, 1965

O. Baboshina, *Skazki Chukotki*, Moscow, 1958

V. Bogoras, *The Chukchee*, Leiden, 1909
'The Eskimo of Siberia', *Memoirs from the American Museum of Natural History*, Vol. 12, 1913
'The Folklore of Northeastern Asia', *American Anthropologist*, Vol. 4, 1902
Koryak Texts', *Publications of the American Ethnological Society*, Vol. 5, 1917

D. Botting, *One Chilly Siberian Morning*, London, 1969

V. Dioszegi, *Popular Beliefs and Folklore Tradition in Siberia*, Hague, 1968

B. Dolgikh, *Skazki i predaniya Nganasan*, Moscow, 1976

G. Ergis, *Yakutskie skazki*, Yakutsk, 1964

V. Jochelson, *Peoples of Asiatic Russia*, The American Museum of Natural History, 1928

I. Khudyakov, *Verkhoyansky sbornik*, Irkutsk, 1890

A. Laptev, 'Skazki Verkhne-Kolymskikh Yukagirov' (unpublished, Yakutsk Academy of Sciences Archives), 1959

V. Leontieva, *Kto samy silny na zemle? Chukotskie skazki*, Magadan, 1974

G. Levi, *Kto samy silny? Skazki narodov Siberii*, Irkutsk, 1975

G. Menovshchikov, *Eskimosskie skazki i legendy*, Magadan, 1969
Skazki i mify narodov Chukotki i Kamchatki, Moscow, 1974

T. Mitlyanskaya, *Khudozhniki Chukotki*, Moscow, 1976

F. Mowat, *The Siberians*, London, 1970

F. Nansen, *Through Siberia, The Land of the Future*, London, 1914

K. Novikova, *Evensky folklor*, Magadan, 1958

Ye. Pomerantseva, *Severnoye siyanie. Skazki narodov severa*, Moscow, 1976

A. Popov, *Yakutsky folklor*, Moscow, 1936

L. Shinkarev, *The Land Beyond the Mountains*, London, 1973

D. Sivtseva-Omolloona, *Yakutskie skazki*, Moscow, 1976

G. Vasilievich, *Istorichesky folklor Evenkov*, Moscow, 1966
Materialy po Evenkyskomu folkloru, Leningrad, 1936

M. Voskoboinikov, *Yazyki i folklor narodov krainevo severa*, Leningrad, 1959

A. Yelagina, *Khozyaika travy. Saamskie skazki*, Moscow, 1973